SILVER FOX

ISBN 978-1-926494-40-1

Silver Fox

MARGARET A. WESTLIE

Selkirk
STORIES

Chapter One

Jane Martin stood looking at the old farmhouse and remembering all the happy summers she had spent there as a child. The old house looks the same as when Grandma and Grandpa lived here. I haven't been here since Grandma went into the home, thought Jane. I saw her as often as I could but she wasn't there very long. It was a sad day when she died. I felt awful about having to put her there, but after her last fall it just wasn't safe for her to live here by herself, and I couldn't be with her all the time.

Her thoughts rambled on. I've lost touch with all the children I used to play with. I mostly played with Ian when he could get out from under his father's thumb. He took an awful ribbing from the other boys for wanting to spend time with me. I wonder where he is now? I heard he went to the Agricultural College in Nova Scotia for awhile. I don't even know if he finished. Maybe he's married with six kids. I doubt that, he was awfully shy back then. I don't even know if I'd recognize him, it has been so long since I've seen him.

She thought back to her school year. It had been

busy with thirty-five fourth graders under her care. I'm glad I have all summer off. This house needs a lot of work. If I do anything with it, I'll need an electrician to check the wiring. Grandpa had it put in shortly after the electricity came out here in the early fifties. I doubt anyone's looked at it since. The last time it was painted, he and Grandma had a row about the colour of the trim. He wanted navy blue and she wanted barn red so it would tie in with the out buildings. They couldn't agree, so Grandpa just went up the ladder one day she when she wasn't home and painted everything white. Jane chuckled at the memory. Grandma wasn't happy about that either, but white it stayed. I think that navy blue would have looked nice and crisp against the white shingles.

A slight movement caught her attention. She looked up at the spare bedroom window and blinked. That curtain is moving. There must be a draft. The curtain stirred itself and seemed to take on a human shape, then moved again and resolved itself into just an old lace curtain. Jane shook her head to clear it. I must be imagining things, she thought.

She took a walk around the front of the house. I'm glad the old sun porch is still there, she thought. I had such fun here with my dolls when I was tiny. When it was hot, Grandma used to let me sleep out here. It was kind of scary when the thunderstorms would roll in. I'm really looking forward to having Lydia here for the summer. She asked if she could bring her dog. Jane tied back her long dark hair with a covered band and continued her wander until supper time, revisiting all the places around the farm that she used to love as a child.

She thought back to a story her mother had told her about Grandma many years ago. It was a strange story, thought Jane. Something about Grandma being an opera singer. I wonder if that was before she met Grandpa? Probably, unless he'd changed an awful lot since before I came along. She thought about her grandfather and his stern Presbyterian ways. No songs except church songs, the Psalms especially. Church every Sunday no matter the weather, except for blizzards. Bible reading every morning before breakfast and again before bed. Hard work. He kept his business to himself. Grandma did too, for that matter, she thought. I don't think she was from here. I don't know why I think that. Her thoughts rambled on. Grandma always smelled of cinnamon and lavender and Grandpa always smelled like the barn and cows. Sometimes he smelled of tobacco smoke but Grandma wouldn't let him smoke indoors. I wonder what they were like when they were young.

After supper Jane washed up and retired to

Grandpa's old chair in the parlour with a book on gardening. The long rays of the setting sun faded into the density of a country night. Somewhere upstairs the sound of a door shutting caught her ear. She looked up from her book. The sound, familiar, but distant in memory, reminded her of something from long ago. She listened intently for a minute or two but the sound did not come again. She shook her head of dark brown curls as if to clear it. Grandma's house was always kind of creaky, she thought, especially when it was windy. She continued to listen a moment longer, then frowned. It's not a windy night, she thought. She listened for another few seconds. The country silence was profound. She shrugged and went back to her book. Another half hour of reading and she was ready for bed.

This was always a creepy old place, she thought. It has so many gables and nooks and crannies for the wind to whistle through. She climbed the stairs. It's a wonder Grandma stayed here after Grandpa died. She sniffed. The smell of Grandpa's wintergreen liniment is still in the air, she thought. She brushed her shiny curls to keep them from tangling too badly while she slept. She sniffed again. Grandma's perfume is still on the air, too. Of course, it's not really that long since they lived here; a couple of years for Grandpa and only a few months for Grandma. She set down her hair brush and climbed into bed. Her firm body, a little stocky like her ancestors, did not fit the hollow in the mattress where her grandmother had slept for all those years. A new box spring and mattress soon, she thought. Sleep came rapidly. I've worked hard today was her final coherent thought before drifting into the softness of sleep.

The sound, when it came again, blended with the creaking of the spruce tree branches just outside the window. The creaking became more urgent and resolved itself into a sound from the parlour where Jane had sat reading with her after supper cup of tea.

Jane came instantly awake and struggled to a sitting position, her eyes wide in the density of the country darkness. There was nothing to see, nothing she could see. I'm glad Lydia is coming to stay for the summer. She'll be here for lunch. The night chill forced her back under the musty smelling quilt. She lay still and listened hard for the next hour. The house seemed to settle itself more comfortably on its foundations.

Silly idea! she thought as fatigue and sleep overtook her again. I'll be glad when Lydia gets here. I hope she brings Charlie. Maybe I should get a dog too. She slept.

The sun, beaming through the space between the curtains, woke her early the next morning. Grandma's drapes never quite fit, she thought in her still sleep-muddled mind. She turned away from the morning brightness and drowsed for a few moments longer. Outside the old rooster crowed. She turned and opened one eye to peer at the clock. "Six o'clock! Be quiet bird, or I'll put you in soup," she muttered. Her thoughts took on more coherency. Her mental list for the day took over and she threw back the covers and headed for the bathroom. I have so much to do today. She splashed water on her face and ran down the list again. Lydia will be here at noon to help, thank goodness.

Jane dressed hurriedly in navy shorts and pale blue T-shirt then ran downstairs. She glanced into the shadowy parlour where she had been sitting the night before. Where did my book go? I thought I left it face down on the side table. She entered the room and threw back the ceiling-high drapery. She stood staring at the now empty table trying to remember what she had actually done with the book. Perhaps I put it on the shelf. She moved over to the dusty book case and began scanning the shelves. It was not there. She frowned, then sneezed and tried to think. Maybe breakfast will help, she thought. Grandma was always losing things like that too. She blamed it on the gremlins. Another survey of the dark panelled room found nothing amiss. Jane glanced at the table one last time noticing for the first time that the dust had been disturbed where she had laid the book. "That's weird," she muttered and headed for the kitchen.

The sunshiny kitchen was cheerier than the parlour had been. The sunlight poured in over the tops of the faded flowered cafe curtains and splashed off the toaster and kettle. She lifted the lid on the kettle to check the water level then began to search the cupboards for something edible for breakfast. I'm glad I brought the toaster from my apartment. I'll have to see what Grandma actually has here.

A creak from the parlour startled her and she stood stalk still, listening hard for a moment. The sound had started almost inaudibly but had increased in intensity until it had caught her attention. She went to the hall door and stood listening for a moment. The creaking continued. She set the coffee mug she had been holding beside her place mat on the table and crept cautiously toward the parlour. She peered around the door jamb and listened. The creaking had stopped. Feeling braver, she stepped into the room and looked around. Nothing seems amiss, she thought, then noticed her book on the side table right where she had left it. Her reading glasses were balanced precariously across the spine. She frowned and went to pick them up and dropped them rapidly. They were too hot to handle. She hovered her hand over the book. It was very warm too. "I don't know what's going on here," she said aloud in her stern school teacher voice, "but if you're playing games, Grandma, I'd like you to stop. It's not funny." She picked up her glasses and stuck them in the neck of her shirt. They had cooled enough to handle.

I'll be glad when Lydia gets here, she thought.

She spent the morning taking inventory of her grandmother's kitchen. She avoided the parlour. There was no more creaking.

She opened a cupboard door. It was crammed with every sized plate for every occasion, some of which Jane had never seen before. Why in the world would she need so many place settings? Some of these are so worn the patterns are indistinguishable. I don't think there's a complete set of anything here. Her thoughts wandered on. She pulled stack after stack of old plates and cups and saucers out and set them on the table. Dust came with every stack. "It's been awhile, Grandma," she muttered. She climbed down off the chair she had been standing on to reach the top shelf and set the last stack in the last space on the counter top. She filled the dishpan with hot soapy water and began washing and thinking, then drying and thinking some more. I think I'll have to decide which set I'm going to keep and take the rest to a resale shop or donate them. I wonder if they're worth anything? Probably not. They never had a lot of spare cash and Grandma was sort of a hoarder. I expect these were all things she picked up at estate sales over the years. There must be about twenty place settings here.

She was just tackling the insides of the cupboards with her wet soapy cloth when Lydia arrived. Jane did not hear her until she spoke.

"Knock, knock!" Lydia Ross called from the porch door, nearly scaring Jane off her precarious perch.

"Oh, you're here!" Jane jumped down off the chair. "I lost track of time."

Lydia pulled out a chair and sat down. "I'm a little early. I left with time to spare because I've never been here before and if I got lost ..." Her voice trailed away as she surveyed what seemed like acres of gleaming dishes. "Did your grandmother entertain a lot?"

Jane filled the kettle and set it on the hot plate, then went in search of the bag of cookies she had bought yesterday. "I didn't think so. Maybe when she was young, but we were never here except for a few weeks in the summertime so she could have had people over every evening. I was here more than Mom and Dad, but there was never any entertaining so I don't really know. I know she always had another place at the table for whoever happened by. Sometimes it would get quite crowded."

"Maybe it was when she was younger," said Lydia. She waved her hand dismissively. "It's lunchtime. I brought some take-out chicken. We should eat it while it's still hot."

Jane poured the boiling water on the teabags in the pot. It was her grandmother's old pot. A yellow one with red and blue flowers and green leaves around the top and across the lid. She glanced at the Grandmother clock on the mantel shelf over the lounge. It had been her grandmother's pride and joy and it groaned and clicked as it tried to chime the hours now. "It is getting late, and I'm getting hungry. I've been at cupboards all morning and there are still more to do."

Lydia jumped up and began setting out Styrofoam containers of the meal. "Will we use some of these plates you've just washed?"

"Sure," said Jane. "What's one more dip in the pan?" She pulled two of the prettier ones off the stacks and found cups and saucers to match. "Did you bring Charlie with you?"

"He's out in the shade watching the squirrels. I staked him. I need to bring him more water. It's kind of warm today." She rose and filled a pitcher with water. "I brought all his dishes and left him with some water when I staked him." She hastened outdoors while Jane pulled the spent teabags from the pot. Presently Lydia was back.

"Do you have someone staying here with you?" She sat and pulled her chair closer to the table.

Jane shook her head. Her dark curls bounced. "No. Why do you ask?"

"Charlie was focused on one of the upstairs windows so I looked too and it seemed as if there was a figure behind the curtains."

Jane frowned. "There's no one here but us chickens. At least as far as I know. We can look when I take you upstairs and show you your room. "

Lunch was long and companionable. Lydia was the grade three teacher at the same school as Jane. She was as blonde as Jane was dark. They had been friends for a long time. News of their mutual friends and colleagues was exchanged and a little gossip was indulged in.

"I'm glad you brought lunch," said Jane. "That was good."

"It's that new place on Great George Street. I'd heard it was good but I'd never tried it. So I took the chance." Lydia rose from her place. "Let's get these dishes done and then you can show me the rest of the place."

A few minutes later they climbed the front stairs together. At the landing Jane flung open the first door on the left. "This is your room. The drapes are 'Grandma specials' all through the house so they let a lot of light in through the cracks. This room will give you the longest lie-in on sunny days." She bent slightly to smooth the coverlet, then frowned and smoothed it again. I don't remember sitting on the bed, she thought, then mentally chased the thought out of her head "My room is across the hall. The door in the middle leads to the attic, but it's locked and I don't know where the key is."

Lydia set her black backpack on the stuffed ladies' chair in the corner then turned to look out the window. "Charlie seems to be enjoying the shade down there."

"D'you like having a dog?"

"They're great company. I talk to him all the time." She turned from the window and allowed the faded gold drapes to fall back into place releasing a shower of dust. She sneezed.

Jane laughed. "I guess I should run those through the air cycle."

"Today's a good day to hang them on the line and give them a beating."

"Bad drapes, eh?" Jane dragged the old wooden chair from the former kitchen set over to the windows and climbed up to begin unhooking the drapes.

Lydia caught them and sneezed again. "You were asking about Charlie."

"Oh, yes." Jane climbed down from the chair and dragged it over to the second window. "I was thinking I might get a dog. I don't know what kind yet, I haven't thought that far."

"Why not get one from the Humane Society?" Lydia stood ready to catch the next dusty drape. "You can get all shapes and sizes, and all ages too."

"M-m-m. I hadn't thought of that. I was thinking breeds, but maybe not. That's where you got Charlie, wasn't it?"

"He was just about to be put down for lack of a taker so I took him. He's the best dog. It's almost as if he knew what his fate was. He was already mostly grown and house broken."

"Don't you have to jump through pet adoption hoops or something?" She dropped the last drape down to Lydia and climbed down from her perch.

"That's just to ensure you'll be good to an animal. Besides, breeds have all kinds of problems and health issues. It's too bad, but humans have done it to them." Lydia gathered the bundle of drapes and headed downstairs. "Where are your clothes pins? I'll put these on the lines. Come to that, where are your lines?"

Jane followed Lydia's slender shape downstairs. "Out here. I'll grab the clothes pins on the way."

Together they wrestled the heavy drapes onto the outdoor lines at the back of the house. "There. A few hours in the breeze will freshen them up. I'm going back to washing cupboards. You can relax."

"Nonsense," said Lydia, "I came here to help, and help I shall. Where's your dust rag and dry mop? I'll start with the windows in my room." She stopped for a moment and looked around herself. "This must have been a big and busy farm when your grandpa was in his prime."

"It was mainly milk and pigs and chickens. The big barn is where he kept the cows at night and the pigs were in the little barn next to it. The loft in the pig barn was where they stored the straw after they threshed. I used to like to go up there and read in the afternoon. The sun used to pour in through the loft door and the straw was soft—well, soft enough." Jane thought about how it was to sleep on. "I remember 'helping' Grandma fill the ticks with straw when I was really little. At least until they finally gave in and bought real mattresses. I think Grandma had to put her foot down over that one. I overheard my mother and father talking about it once. As frugal as Grandma was, Grandpa could outdo her almost every time."

Together they walked around the rest of the farm-yard. "The chicken coop was at the end of the little barn and the woodshed was next to that."

"What are those odd looking boxes? Rabbit hutches?" asked Lydia.

"Grandpa kept foxes while they were in demand. They were beautiful, all silvery grey with a dark overlay of fur. I don't know if you ever heard about the big fox industry that was going away back when?"

"I heard something about it once. But I didn't really take it in. Dad was reading The Guardian and he was quite upset about the decline in the fur industry. He said something about a lot of people being ruined by it, and thank goodness he hadn't put any money into it when his brother asked him to."

"Well, Grandpa came out of that okay. He saw the market trend and the prices declining and he sold out early. He was pretty canny."

"Sounds like he was," said Lydia. She lost interest in the past as they reached the back door. "So where are the dusters and rags?" Jane handed Lydia the required items and she disappeared upstairs. Jane filled the dishpan with fresh soapy water and took up where she had left off when Lydia had arrived. After half an hour Lydia came downstairs. "Have you got some more cleaning rags? Those hall windows could use a good clean while I'm at it."

"In the cupboard in the porch where I got the others. Just open the top drawer and you'll find them." Jane picked up the dishtowel and began drying the latest round of dishes.

Lydia returned with her hands full of rags. "Paper towel?"

Jane nodded in the direction of the towel holder. "Take that one. Just bring it back when you're finished."

Lydia pulled the paper roll out of its holder and stuck it under her left elbow, then disappeared upstairs again. She was back a short time later with all her cleaning supplies. "Shall I just dump this outdoors?"

"On the garden." Jane began stacking clean dishes into their clean spaces in the cupboard.

Lydia returned in a moment with her empty bucket. She sat in the rocker in the bay window to rest. "By the way, I dusted the library as I was passing. You really need to take all those books off the shelves and give that a good clean out too. Who was the old lady in there reading?"

"What old lady?" Jane swung around in alarm.

The air seemed to thicken and a cold shiver ran down Jane's back. "There are no old ladies here that I know of." She frowned.

Lydia gave a tiny shrug. "I don't know. She looked up when I came in and said something to me that I didn't quite catch. Something about a coat. I turned to set down the bucket and move a few things off the table. When I turned back she was gone." Lydia shuddered. "It was really kind of spooky. She didn't make any noise, and she didn't go past me. I would have known if she had. The only sound was the creaky rocker."

"What did she look like?" Jane almost stared at Lydia.

"Kind of old-fashioned. Her hair was in finger waves like the old ladies wore when they were young. She wasn't grey though." Lydia furrowed her brow trying to bring the image of the woman back into focus. "Come to think of it, I couldn't really see her and she was very hard to hear."

"She doesn't sound like anyone from around here." Jane filled the kettle to boil. "She might have been a friend of Grandma's. She always had people coming and going. Sometimes they'd stay for the day, sometimes not. Some she didn't even know, I think they may have been friends of Grandpa's." She was silent for a moment. "But that doesn't make any sense. Why would she be here? How did she get in?" Jane thought back to the disappearing glasses and book from the night before.

"Wasn't that dangerous just to invite strangers in for a meal?" asked Lydia.

Jane pulled off the light blue sweatband that she had confined her curls with and shook her head. "Grandma didn't think so. Of course, once Grandpa died she didn't do it as much. With no man about the place and living away out here, it really wasn't safe." She sat down to rest for a moment. "I'm glad that job is done. It has never been my favourite thing to do." Presently the kettle began bubbling and she rose to set the tea. "So that's two and a half rooms completed. Want a cookie?" Jane reached for the bag of cookies. "By the way, I checked the other rooms when you went to get the bucket and there was no one there."

The next morning Jane rolled out of bed just as the sun came round the edge of the curtain. She even got ahead of the rooster. She groaned as her morning stretch revealed the sore spots from all her cleaning efforts yesterday. I guess I'm not in as good a shape as I thought. Her mind rambled on. What will I do today? she thought. More cleaning and I must see if there's anything in the garden. I don't know if Grandma planted anything this spring or not. She was still pretty spry so she may have. Jane crept downstairs so as not to waken Lydia.

She quietly closed the kitchen door behind herself then turned to discover Lydia asleep in the rocker with Charlie at her feet. The down comforter from the bedroom behind the kitchen was wrapped snugly around her, and Charlie kept watch from the tail of it at her feet. He 'wuffed' at Jane's entrance and wagged the tip of his tawny tail. Lydia stirred.

"What's the matter, Charlie? Time to go out?" Lydia opened her eyes. "Oh, is it morning already? What time is it?"

"It's six o'clock and what are you doing sleeping in the rocker? It wasn't the mattress was it? I didn't test it and Grandma was very saving, so it's pretty old."

Lydia untangled herself from the comforter. "No, it wasn't the mattress, it was Charlie. He wouldn't come upstairs with me last night. He didn't want to go past the parlour door. And he didn't want me to either. I don't know what got into him. He braced himself and just would not go past, and he's too big a dog for me to pick up and carry. He was very agitated and I was afraid if I forced the issue he might snap at me."

"That's odd." Jane squatted down to ruffle Charlie's floppy beige ears. "What's up with that, Charlie?"

"I don't know," said Lydia, "but whatever it is, he'd better get over it." She began folding the comforter. "He needs to go out. You're dressed, will you take him?"

Jane picked up Charlie's leash and clipped it onto his collar. "C'mon, Charlie, let's go." She opened the kitchen door into the porch and led Charlie outside. The screen door slapped and rattled behind her. It was a familiar sound. She stood for a moment absorbing the clear brightness of the summer morning and breathing in the fresh, salt-tangy air from the Strait. She let out the retractable leash so that Charlie could have a wander and some privacy for his 'business.' To her right was the garden with a good green growth over most of it. I hope those are plants and not weeds, she thought. The garden is huge. It's a wonder that Grandma had the strength. Maybe one of the neighbour kids helped her. Presently Lydia joined her.

"We can tether Charlie to the chain under the tree when he comes back." She took the leash from Jane. "That'll keep him out from underfoot while we work this morning."

"I wonder whatever got into him last night? I thought you came up right after me."

Lydia dug her bare toes into the soft sand by the side of the lane. "I have no idea. When I went to leave the kitchen after I turned out the light, he came to the threshold and whined. I coaxed him to come and after awhile I managed to get him into the hall but after that he refused to budge. I tried to pull him by his collar but no luck, he just sat down on his haunches and refused to go any farther. He didn't want me to leave him alone either. When I gave up and headed upstairs you should have heard him cry. It was if he was afraid. I've never known him to be like this. So I went and got the comforter from the bedroom behind the kitchen and wrapped up in that. It seemed to satisfy him and he quieted down."

"We should see if he'll go past the parlour in the daytime," said Jane. "It's kind of a shadowy place at night, maybe that's what has him spooked."

"Maybe. We can try him later. Right now, all I'm interested in is breakfast." Lydia walked in the direction of the stretched leash. "C'mon, Charlie, let's get you settled for the morning."

After breakfast Jane hung the damp tea towel on the wooden drying arms behind the old wood stove. There was no need of a fire in the summer but it was closer and more convenient than the big clothes line outdoors. "Shall we try Charlie and the parlour in daylight now?"

Lydia jumped to her feet and set her empty mug

on the counter beside the tea pot. "No time like the present." She stuck her bare feet into sandals and picked up Charlie's leash. "I'll get him." She headed outdoors to find Charlie huddled as far under the tree as he could get. He was staring at the upstairs window and whining. Lydia turned to look in the direction he was staring. To her perception, the curtains on her own bedroom window moved slightly in the morning breeze. There was a strange stillness to the air. Charlie's golden hackles raised and a low, barely audible growl emanated from his throat. The air felt electric. He leaned against Lydia's legs and whined.

"What are you looking at, you silly dog?"

"Wuff!" said Charlie and tried to bury his face in her sandals.

Lydia sat down on the grass beside him and began watching the window. The breeze disturbed the curtains again. Lydia thought she discerned a womanly form in their shadows. She stared harder and the shadows resolved themselves into curtains again. Lydia shook her head. "We're both being silly, you and I."

Charlie whined and leaned against Lydia's side.

"C'mon you, it's time to go and find out what this is." Lydia rolled to her feet just as Jane joined her.

"What what is?" asked Jane.

Lydia made a slight face of exasperation. "Charlie's spooked again. He was staring at the upstairs window so I thought I'd look too, but all I could see was the curtains moving in the breeze." She bent to attach Charlie's leash. "Although, I must say, they did create shadows as if someone were standing there." She straightened and tugged at the leash then shivered slightly. "Let's go and put an end to this nonsense, once and for all."

Charlie hung his head and tucked his tail but followed Lydia into the house. He whined as they crossed the threshold and held back a little.

Jane got behind him and pushed his dark golden rump into the kitchen. A slight movement out the corner of her eye caught her attention but there was nothing there. She frowned. "That's funny!" She peered at the tray of clean dishes. "The dishes are washed and they're draining on the rack."

"What's funny about that?" asked Lydia.

"I didn't do the dishes. I came right outside after I brushed my teeth and made my bed." She picked one up to inspect for cleanliness. "It's hot! It's as if it has just been rinsed!" She turned, wide-eyed to Lydia.

"D'you have ghosts?"

"Not that I know of. Grandma used to keep some weird visitors from time to time but she never mentioned anything strange, like ghosts."

Lydia shrugged. "We'll keep an eye on the dishes

tomorrow morning and see if they get done. In the meantime, we have our hands full with Charlie."

She led the way toward the hallway with a nervous Charlie at her heel. He whined at the threshold and seemed about to baulk but Jane was close behind him and he had to keep moving. He flattened himself against the wall opposite the parlour door and whined again. Jane glanced into the parlour and gasped.

"The chair is rocking all by itself!"

Lydia looked too. She stared and blinked. "That's the old lady I saw upstairs this morning. She's the same one I saw here yesterday too. What is going on in your house, Jane? Is that your grandmother?"

Jane stared hard at the independently rocking chair trying to discern a source for the movement but could not. "I don't know what's going on, but I intend to find out." She let go of Charlie's shivering rump and turned toward the parlour door. Charlie whined and retreated to the kitchen as close to the outside door as he could get. Jane took a stance in the parlour door with her hands on her hips. "Who are you? What do you want?" Her tone was forceful, almost angry. Although she still could see no one and nothing in the chair except a faint mistiness, it stopped rocking. She advanced a step into the room and demanded: "What's going on here?" Her book, still lying on the side table from yesterday took on a life of its own and sailed straight at her head. She ducked as it whizzed past her right ear and bounced off the hall wall landing at Lydia's feet. She fled to the kitchen dragging Lydia with her. A faint chuckle followed them.

"What was that?" Lydia collapsed into the rocking chair in the kitchen alcove. Charlie whined at the door and cast a look of doggie despair in her direction.

For want of anything better to do, Jane filled the kettle and set it to boil. She kept a close eye on what she could see of the parlour door. The creak of the living room rocker continued, perhaps even louder than before. For certain it was faster.

Jane cleared her throat. "I guess I really riled whoever that used to be." She gave a weak giggle.

Charlie whined again.

"I'll take him outdoors," said Lydia. She rose and picked up Charlie's leash.

"Not without me you won't," said Jane. She led the way outdoors into the sanity of sunshine and clear morning.

Lydia bent to clip Charlie's collar to the long lead she had tethered him to. "What are we going to do?"

"It's really not your problem, Lydia. I wouldn't blame you if you wanted to go home and never come back. If you do, take Charlie with you. He's not much of a guard dog." Jane sighed. "I'm sorry. I shouldn't have said that, at least not like that." She sighed again.

"You're right, he isn't," said Lydia. "But he's going to learn, because I'm not going to leave you here on your own. What do you think?"

"I'm not very brave either. I've never known this house to be so spooky, at least not while Grandma lived here. I don't know what's going on." Jane sat down on the grass and stared at the windows. She had left the windows upstairs open to air the bedrooms, and a fresh breeze straight off the Northumberland Strait ruffled the curtains. Jane shivered. "I can see why those curtains look like someone is standing there."

Lydia sat down on the grass beside Jane. Charlie, as big as he was, tried to sit in her lap. Lydia looked in the direction that Jane was gazing. "I see what you mean." She pushed Charlie off her lap and sat silently for a moment then said: "Let's set the cleaning aside for today and take a road trip. I'll drive. We'll take a picnic and go somewhere where Charlie can run off the leash for awhile. You'd like that wouldn't you, Charlie?"

Charlie wuffed and wagged the tip of his tail.

"We'll drive up to East Point and have our picnic and sit on the sand and puzzle things out."

"That'll take us most of the day up and back,"

said Jane. "Maybe things will settle themselves down by then."

"Maybe," said Lydia. "My cousin says she can see things and she says it all depends on what they want. If it's urgent enough they won't stop until they get it. They have even been known to start fires or hide things. They can definitely disrupt the household."

The picnic at East Point eased their nerves, and Charlie ran himself tired on the beach. He frolicked in and out of the water and up and down the beach until he collapsed, wet and exhausted, between Lydia and Jane and yawned. He dropped his head on his paws and closed his eyes.

"Phew, you stink, Charlie," said Jane. She leaned back on her elbows and rubbed his ears. "It's bath time for you before I let you into the house tonight." She stared off to the horizon misted by distance and sea air. "I wonder what Grandma thought she was doing, letting people stay with her? I don't think she even knew half of them."

"I dunno," said Lydia. She rolled onto her belly and began to watch an ant dragging a bit of seaweed across the sand. The sun was warm on her legs and back. "People were more hospitable then."

"Mm hm," said Jane. "More trusting too, I think."

She continued to stare out to sea. "I know I wouldn't do it."

"Your grandfather was still living then, wasn't he?"

"Yeah, but he'd have been no help if anything had gone wrong." Jane laughed. "He'd have probably met them at the gate and invited them in for a drink."

"Was he fond of the booze, then?"

"It could be said," replied Jane. "He liked a *ceilidh*, but for all that they never went without, and he was never a mean drunk." She sat up and began to scoop sand through her fingers. The dryness of it sifted through her hands and was picked up by the slight breeze off the gulf. It dusted away down the beach. She thought of her grandfather in silence for a few minutes. "I don't know where he got his money from. The relatives used to say he was suspected of rum running during Prohibition." She went quiet for a moment. "I don't know. It could have been just talk."

"You've never come across old journals or anything like that have you?" asked Lydia.

Jane shook her head. "I have never been a rummager. I was taught a very strong sense of boundaries around possessions when I was a child. I wouldn't have dared. Even now I don't like going through Grandma's things." She stared off to the horizon remembering the one and only scolding Grandma had ever given her. The severity of it and the shame she felt was still with her. She mentally chased the memory out of her mind.

"Never bothered me," said Lydia. "I thought nothing of snooping. How else was I supposed to find out? They never told us anything."

"You sound kind of disgruntled still."

"I hate secrecy." Lydia rolled over and sat up. "Privacy is fine. I have no problem with that, but whispering in the corners and shutting up when anyone came within earshot is just plain wrong."

"It's usually just gossip anyway, isn't it?" said Jane.

"The family was just like that when my aunt died. The cousins used to always play together, and then all of a sudden amidst all the whispering we weren't allowed to play together anymore. It created a terrible rift and it has never been the same since, and I'm still not sure why."

"Is that why the cousin you occasionally mention is never in the picture?"

"Mm," said Lydia. "I guess so. We're of the same age and we always had fun, but everything has changed now. We're not the same people anymore. I don't even know what to talk to her about."

"That's sad." Jane stroked Charlie's silky ears. His tawny fur had dried and he was soft and pleasant to the touch. The briny smell had dissipated somewhat too. "How is she different?"

"She's into all kinds of spooky stuff now. Ghosts and spirits. She really believes it all. She claims she can read auras too. Whatever they are."

Jane laughed. "You're afraid she can read you too, huh?"

"You never know, and I don't want to find out."

They sat in silence for awhile until the breeze turned abruptly cooler and dark clouds started rolling in. Jane shivered. "I guess this is the end of our picnic." She rolled to her feet and began repacking the basket.

"Fun while it lasted," said Lydia. She began folding the blanket. Charlie whined and stretched front and back. She snapped the leash on him. "You're not going for another dip in the ocean. We don't let wet dogs ride with us." Charlie sat down on his haunches.

Together they hurried up the slope just as the first raindrops began to fall.

The house remained quiet for the rest of the week. Jane and Lydia avoided any cleaning in the parlour and tried to walk past the door without looking in. Together they managed to turn out closets and freshen drapery and wash bed covers upstairs. The musty old house smell dissipated except in the parlour. Jane tried not to think of the eerie events of the past week.

"You know, I have to be gone for next week," said Lydia. "I have relatives coming and I can't get out of it." She rose from her chair by the kitchen table and poured herself another cup of tea.

Jane's heart fell a little. "I wasn't thinking about that if I could help it. I know you'll be back after they've gone."

Lydia sat down and set her cup to cool slightly before trying it. "They're from Ontario and they'll need a place to stay and some entertaining. I think they're flying down, so they won't have their car. I'll have to be doing some taxiing around."

"Why don't you bring them out here?" Hope shone in Jane's eyes.

"I don't think that would work. They're not comfortable to have around. Auntie Maude can be a tyrant and Uncle George is an old fuss budget. They've always deserved each other to my way of thinking. Besides, with all the weird stuff going on here just now, you definitely don't want them around."

"When you come back here after, bring your spooky cousin – and Charlie?" Jane toyed with the handle of her cup.

Lydia smiled. She reached across the table and

patted Jane's arm. "Charlie's not much help. But I'll come again next week and stay like we planned. If I can find Gertrude, I'll see what she's doing and bring her too. Will you be okay on your own?"

"I don't plan to spend a whole lot of time in the house. I need to attend to my apartment and bring some of my things out here if I'm going to live here. I haven't entirely made up my mind. I'll have to give my notice in at the housing office a month ahead so I'll have to have decided by the end of August."

"That's two months away so you have plenty of time to decide," said Lydia. "D'you think that things will settle down by then?"

Jane sighed. "I don't know. Whoever she is, she has been quiet all week, though I'm not looking forward to spending time here by myself next week." She sighed again. "I'll keep busy. Maybe that will keep things quiet."

A faint chuckle echoed from somewhere.

Chapter Two

The week seemed long and dreary. It rained almost every day. The lane to the road was a red swamp, with potholes filled with red water that Jane could just about float a dory in. Because of the cloud cover, night seemed to fall early and she was forced to stay indoors most of the evening. She kept on house cleaning long after dark just to keep her mind from straying to the presence in the parlour.

I wish Lydia were here, she thought. She gave herself a mental shake. I'm letting whoever that is in the parlour take over the house. Maybe I should just move the rocker. Put it out in the barn. I'm going to sit in there this evening and read. No more retreating to the kitchen. A knock sounding at the kitchen door made her jump.

I don't think ghosts can knock on doors so I guess it must be human, she thought. She swung the door open and flipped on the porch light. It was a tall man dressed in a raincoat and sou'wester. His truck was parked in the shelter of the spruce trees by the lane. He carried a small basket of eggs in one hand and with his other hand he was poised to knock again.

"Oh," said Jane. "Who are you?" He smells good, she thought in the periphery of her mind. He looks as if he got cleaned up for a date. He looks sort of familiar.

The man stuck out his hand. "I'm Ian. We knew each other when we were kids. I live the next farm down. I had some extra eggs I thought you might be able to use. I wanted to see if you had drowned yet." He ducked his head shyly then set the eggs on the table beside the door and turned to go.

"Oh," said Jane again. "Thank you, and, no, I haven't drowned yet, though it might not be long." She stared up at the man as if she had never seen one of their species before. "Will you come in for a cup?"

The man's expression brightened. He pulled off his sou'wester and raincoat and hung them on the hook behind the outside door. "I don't suppose you have a cookie too?"

Jane stood aside to allow him into the kitchen. "Store bought is all I have. Will that do?"

Ian sat down at the table. "That will do nicely, thank you." He looked around. The kitchen shone in the light. The evening dishes stood draining in the rack, Jane's grandmother's wood stove shone with stove black and the old kettle, polished to brightness, reflected it all. He nodded appreciatively and cleared his throat. "I see you've been working hard. Do you intend to live here?"

Jane lifted mugs from the cupboard and set them on the table. "I hope to. I can't afford to keep it up if I'm paying rent in town too. It seems the most practical thing to do. I'll save money in the long run."

"Good," said Ian, then lapsed into silence. He ran his hand through his wavy hair and cleared his throat as if to say something then didn't.

Jane set out the plate of cookies. "You would have known my grandmother."

"She was one of my favourite people. I did the garden for her these last few years. I have the machines that can make quick work of the ground in the spring. She kept up with the planting and weeding herself."

"She was amazing." Jane brought out the milk and sugar and set them on the table. "So did she keep the garden this spring too?"

"Not as much. I had to help her a lot. She still liked to do her own canning. I put in the rest of it just before you arrived just to please her. I knew she wouldn't be home again after that last fall."

"Where did she keep the jars?" Jane sat down opposite him and pushed the plate of cookies nearer to him. She looked at him intently and thought: He's grown into a nice looking man. Looks like one of the old Scottish farmers, sort of rosy in his cheeks. The observation was brief. I like the look of you but staring is rude. She glanced down.

"In the cellar. Have you not been down?" Ian bit into a cookie.

Jane shook her head. "I haven't gotten there yet."

"Would you like me to fetch you some pickles or jam?" Another bite and the cookie was gone. "If you have a flashlight I could go down tonight and see what's there. Otherwise it'll have to wait until tomorrow."

"There's no light down there?"

Ian reached for another cookie. "Not even one bulb."

"I'm surprised. They had the electricity put in after it came to the Island. It was pretty basic. One light per room. I wonder why they didn't have one put down there?"

Ian shook his head. "I've never been able to figure that one out either. They may have gotten the idea that any more bulbs would be too expensive. Your grandfather was pretty saving. The fuse box is there in the porch. It wouldn't have been difficult to run a line. They needed a new box with proper circuit breakers, but I could never convince them."

Jane sighed. "I suppose I'd better have the wiring checked out before too long. Dear knows what they'll find. It's probably not even up to code anymore."

"Not likely," said Ian. "Is your friend coming back?"

"Yes. She has company this week. Why?" Jane watched her visitor as if to assess the motive of his question.

Ian ducked his head again. "I wanted to see you."

"How I turned out, huh?" Jane suppressed a chuckle.

Ian rose. "If you have that flashlight handy, I could go and get you those preserves."

After Ian had returned with a jar of each kind of preserve he pulled on his raincoat and sou'wester. "I must be off. The rooster crows pretty early these days. If you decide to investigate the cellar, be careful. Those stairs are steep and the treads are narrow." He looked down at Jane's long, slender feet in their slippers. "Put your shoes on too. No telling what's down there without good lighting."

"I'll call the electrician this week," said Jane. "Thanks for the eggs. I might get a little baking done now."

Jane locked the door behind Ian and returned to the kitchen to set their mugs in the sink and tidy the kitchen. He has turned into a very nice man, she thought. I like how his chestnut hair kind of waves and curls around his ears although he does need a haircut. A little shy, I think. I'm glad, for the moment, that Lydia wasn't here. She looked at the clock. Eight-thirty. I guess I could still read awhile, she thought. She sighed. I don't want to go into the parlour but I can't let the ghosties get the better of me. She stood staring at the parlour door for a moment longer. "Nonsense! There're no such things as ghosts," she muttered. "And even if there were, they'd still be just ghosts." She poured out the last of the tea into a fresh mug and headed toward the hall. Besides, my book is in there and so are my glasses.

She flipped on the overhead light by the doorway and stood for a moment surveying the parlour. The rocking chair swayed gently in the alcove as if someone were sitting in it, or had just been sitting in it. Jane shivered. Nonsense! She thought again. She sat down in her chair by the little table and turned on the lamp. She settled herself into the wing chair and arranged her own curves into the curves left by her grandfather. It had been his chair and she didn't quite fit. But I like the smell of it, she thought. It smells of his pipe tobacco, wintergreen and that barny smell he always seemed to carry with him even after he'd had a bath. She squirmed into a more comfortable position and began to read.

A good book usually held her attention completely, but tonight she couldn't seem to concentrate. She could see the rocking chair swaying out of the corner of her eye and hear its creak on the old floor boards. She hitched her chair a little to block out the sight but couldn't avoid the creak, creak, creak of the rocking chair. Finally, after about half an hour, she gave up and returned to the kitchen. She settled herself into the rocking chair in the kitchen alcove and began to read. The creak from the parlour became more insistent. Jane set her book aside and stomped into the hallway. She peered into the shadows of the parlour. There appeared to be a glow emanating from the old rocker. It continued to sway in the gloom and the creaking continued.

"Oh, stop it!" said Jane loudly. "Just stop it!"

The creaking stopped abruptly and the chair came to a standstill as the glow brightened and dimmed.

"Oh!" Jane stared at it. The glow was still there. She decided to be a little more polite. "Please, just go away."

Whispers gathered in her mind but she couldn't quite hear what they were. "Please leave me alone." She seemed rooted to her place in the parlour doorway. "I don't know who you are, or what you want, but whatever it is, I don't have it."

The glow seemed to brighten and then dim as if it understood what she had just said. Jane felt her feet release themselves and she turned and hurried back to the kitchen, just as the lights flickered and went out.

Damn! thought Jane. Just what I need, a power failure. I'm calling the electrician tomorrow. She fumbled around in the dark for the flashlight that Ian had used earlier. It was in the drawer where she had put it after he left. She went out to the porch to look at the fuse box and discovered the rows of glass fuses, none of which seemed to have blown, and none of which were labelled. She jiggled each one and finally light was restored. I have to get this changed, she thought. I also have to get Lydia back here.

It was a week before Lydia returned. She brought Charlie. She looked very tired.

"What happened to you? You look exhausted."

Lydia pulled out a kitchen chair and collapsed into it. "I am. Auntie Maude and Uncle George are so demanding. Take me here. Take me there. Get me this. Do that. You didn't do that right, so I'd have to do things all over again. They didn't like what I offered them to eat. I'm not the cook my mother was."

"But your mother wasn't a very good cook," said Jane.

"Yeah, but try and tell them that. I hope they stay in Ontario next year. I'm beat. Have you made tea yet today?"

"The kettle's on. Put your feet up and tell me what you did for them." Jane pushed another chair around so Lydia could put her feet up. "It's a wonder they had the stamina to keep going. They're pretty old, aren't they?"

"Not so old. Just over sixty, and you know what they say, sixty is the new forty."

"So they're very apt to be back next year."

"Mm hm." Lydia sighed. "Very likely."

Charlie settled his head on his paws and snorted as if he didn't like what he was hearing.

Jane laughed. "Even Charlie has had enough."

"That was the other thing. They didn't like Charlie and wanted me to keep him outdoors."

"But you live in an apartment building!" Jane stopped pouring water on the tea bags and looked at Lydia. "How could you keep him outdoors?"

"That's just it, I couldn't." She looked over at Charlie. "Poor Charlie has had just as hard a week as I have. They wanted me to board him while they were there."

"I hope you refused."

"I did. I drew the line at banishing Charlie, but I had to keep him out of the way. The only time we had any alone time was when I walked him. They stayed away then."

"Well, it's all over now. We can pamper Charlie all he wants. I bought some Greenies when I was at the store the other day. I hope he likes them."

"He'll like them. Anything food related and he's happy."

"Let me tell you what I've been doing." Jane pulled the tea bags and filled the yellow mugs. She set them on the table and pushed one to within Lydia's reach. "My neighbour next door came by. I used to play with him when we were little. His name is Ian." She pulled out a chair opposite Lydia and settled herself onto the quilted chair pad. "He's been helping Grandma all these years."

Lydia added milk to her tea and gave it a stir. "What's he like?"

"Shy. He didn't stay long. Just a half hour or so." Jane blew on her tea to cool it. "He's turned out very nice. He brought me a basket of eggs. It was pouring rain out and there he was, in sou'wester and slicker, and rubber boots practically up to his knees."

"You let him in? No questions asked?" Lydia put her feet on the floor with a thump and hitched her chair closer to the table.

Jane shrugged. "I recognized him as someone I used to know and our childhood escapades came back to me when he reminded me. It's been years and we've both grown up. I barely remember any of the children from around here. I offered him a cup of tea and he accepted. He told me he used to help Grandma with the garden."

"You need to get yourself a dog." Lydia held out her cup for a refill. Charlie whined from the alcove.

"Oops, I forgot his dog treat." Jane rose and and rummaged in the cupboard. Charlie barked. "Hold your horses, there, Charlie. I'm sorry to be so slow and forgetful. It's my age, don't you know." Jane ripped open the bag and tossed a bone shaped treat in Charlie's direction. He caught it mid-air. Jane closed the bag and returned it to the cupboard then poured them each another cup of tea. "Want a cookie with that?"

"No, thanks, I'm cookied out." Lydia added milk to her steaming cup.

"It's just as well. I don't have any. I gave the last ones to Ian the other evening."

"Auntie Maud and Uncle George ate cookies morning, noon and night. I could hardly keep up."

Jane laughed. "It's a wonder they're not diabetic."

"They are, but that doesn't stop them and they're both as fat as pigs. Auntie Maude won't share a bed with Uncle George anymore, there's not enough room."

"What did they do?"

"One in one room and one on the couch. It was the best I could do."

"Well, they're gone back to Ontario now."

"I think I'm going to make an excuse not to have them next year." Lydia sipped her tea in silence for a few minutes. "By the way, how was your house guest while I was away?"

"D'you mean my ghost?" Jane's face took on weary lines. "Still rocking and glowing."

"Glowing?"

"Yeah. I spoke sharply to her the other evening and she didn't like it."

"She must think this is her house."

"I dunno. I told her straightforwardly that I didn't know what she wanted, and whatever it was, I didn't have it." Jane frowned. "I also told her to go away."

"And did she?" Lydia leaned forward on her elbows, excitement in her bright blue eyes.

"Not right away. I could still hear the rocking chair squeaking on the wooden floor after I came out here. That was last night, so we'll know tonight if she stayed away."

"Why don't you just come back to town?"

"I'm stubborn, I guess. This house used to be a delightful place and now ... " Jane's voice trailed away. She sighed and looked around the gleaming kitchen. "I haven't had a good sleep since you left. It poured rain night and day for half the week so I couldn't go out. Ian has been my only visitor and he was only here for less than an hour. I didn't tell him about the 'lady' visitor. Between the rain and the ghosts, the atmosphere was just thick and heavy and I couldn't do anything about any of it."

"I guess rain doesn't bother her. Wherever she comes from." Lydia sat back on her chair and put her feet up on the other chair again.

Jane sighed. "We've certainly had enough of that this past week."

"I was worried about driving through the big puddle at the end of the lane. It's practically a lake."

"I need the lane graded and another load of gravel on it. I don't think it has been touched since Grandpa died. Not that he ever did much about it except drag it." Jane rose from her seat. "What do you fancy for supper?"

"Salad." Lydia gave a small moan. "I cannot face another heavy meal. I think I might just hate food."

"Salad it is. D'you want some steak cut up in it? I got a lovely steak at the butcher's yesterday."

"Sounds wonderful. No cookies though."

The next morning dawned sunny and warm. It was the best day so far that summer. Jane took her teacup outdoors while she surveyed her little realm. Charlie tagged along. He snuffled his way around the yard and barked at a squirrel. It chattered at him from the high branch to which it had retreated. The sun felt warm and penetrating on Jane's back. She revelled in the warmth. Her steps took her past the garden. I wonder if Grandma had anything planted here this spring, she thought. Jane bent to inspect the rows. Carrots! Lots of them, she thought. Grandma certainly believed in abundance.

Jane sat back on her heels and remembered the smell of baking emanating from the kitchen. Cinnamon and cloves and ginger. It was like perfume, thought Jane. The cookie jar was always filled. Grandpa particularly liked those big molasses ones. He always put a thick coating of butter on the back of them. Grandma used to chide him about eating too much butter. Her sugar cookies with a raisin on top were always my favourite. I'd eat around the raisin and save it until last. It always tasted a little burnt but that didn't matter.

Jane got to her feet and walked the next row. Look at the Swiss chard. It's huge! I wonder if I could freeze some of it. It'll be good this summer even if I can't. Half a row of cabbage and the other half of turnip. Jane chuckled to herself. I wonder if that will be enough, Grandma.

Presently Lydia joined her. "It's certainly a big garden." She bent to snap the long leash to Charlie's collar.

"She believed in plenty, and plenty is what she

always had. Sometimes it was only leftovers but there was always room at the table for whoever stopped by. She'd say: 'Stay. I'll just put another potato in the pot.' And there'd be one or two more for dinner. They always had dinner at noon." Jane thought back to all the people she'd met around the kitchen table. "I met people from all walks of life. Doctors, lawyers, farmers and fishermen. Probably a rum runner or two as well, if the stories about my grandfather are true. Of course, they'd never tell."

"Is anything ready to harvest yet?" asked Lydia.

Jane bent down to inspect the carrots. "Some carrots, if we take the biggest ones. There's lots of chard too. I bought a little chicken at the butcher's too. I'll make us a chicken dinner."

"With gravy?" Lydia looked hopeful.

"Pints of it. Enough left over to make soup. I'll make us a pie too. Ian left me with lots of eggs, and I see the rhubarb is ready to be harvested. I can make a rhubarb custard pie. I wonder if I have any tapioca." Jane rose to her feet. "If I'm going to do all that this morning I'd better get started."

She hurried toward the house. "Did you leave the door open?"

Lydia shook her head. "I didn't think so. We don't need an invasion of flies."

Jane cautiously entered and looked around. No one was visible. There was no one in the kitchen or the parlour either. She picked up the poker for the stove and crept up the stairs. No one was there either. I guess it just didn't latch right. We'll have to be careful of that or we will have flies, she thought. She turned to go back downstairs. Lydia stood at the bottom staring at the steps.

"What's the matter?" Jane started down the steps.

"No! Wait!" Lydia continued to stare.

Jane stopped on the second step, her right foot poised to take the third one. She hastily drew it back. "What is it?"

"Footprints." Lydia seemed fixed to the spot.

"Footprints?" Jane looked at the next few steps, then checked the bottoms of her shoes. They were dry. She made her way down the remaining steps, avoiding the center where the muddy footprints were. She turned and looked at them. They were small, neat and bare, unlike her long slender feet. "Those aren't mine. I'm wearing sandals."

They stared at one another for a moment then looked back at the muddy prints. They were still there. "Charlie?" said Jane.

Lydia shook her head. "He's on the leash in the yard. Besides, he won't go past the parlour door without an escort. Anyway, they look human. They look like a child's." She continued to stare at the muddy footprints. "I think I need to call cousin Gertrude and her boss."

They turned as one and headed back to the kitchen. As they passed the parlour door the rocking chair began to creak and a faint giggle seemed to echo in their inner ears. In the yard Charlie howled.

Jane collected the rag mop, still a little damp from scrubbing the kitchen floor yesterday. She marched back to the stairs with the mop held under her arm like a lance, then stood stalk still staring at the stair steps. There were no footprints to scrub. She could feel waves of heat and cold suffuse her being. "Lydia!" She managed a nervous squeak, then cleared her throat. "Lydia!" she shouted. "C'mere!"

In seconds Lydia was beside her. "What ... ?" She swallowed audibly as she stood staring at the steps. "You did a quick job of those."

"But I didn't. " Jane lowered the mop. "I never touched the stairs."

Lydia frowned. "They just disappeared?"

Jane nodded and continued to stare as if she could force the muddy footprints to reappear. "There's something weird about this house." She backed away from from the stairs still holding the mop in lance position.

Back in the sunshine of the kitchen they considered their situation. "I don't know if I want to sleep here tonight," said Jane. "I've never been afraid when Grandma was alive but now ..."

"D'you want to go back to town? We could be there in a half hour. I know it'll please Charlie."

"I want to know what's going on." Jane leaned the mop in corner and pulled out a chair. "I never believed much in haunted houses or ghosts. I always thought they were a figment of overactive imaginations, but now I'm beginning to wonder."

Lydia shook her head in disbelief. "I'd like to know too. I was brought up in a household that was inactive as far as church and spiritual ideas were concerned, so I have little concept of the afterlife or even if there is one. I just don't think of it much."

"Me neither. I've been to so many churches over the years I don't know what to believe. I know it's certainly not what they all thought they were teaching. I always came away feeling spiritually starved."

"Hm," said Lydia. "I never got that close. I guess I see what's happening all around me and wonder how God can let this happen."

"Well, this is my house and I will not have ghosties living in it." Jane nodded adamantly just as the creaking from the parlour became louder and a cackle of laughter filled the air.

Lydia and Jane turned as one toward the hall door. "T-that was real enough," said Lydia.

Jane jumped to her feet and hastened to the parlour door. The laughter came again and the rocking chair rocked by itself in the bay window. Jane stared hard. There seemed to be a glow surrounding it. It faded as she stared until it was as if it had never been. Outside, Charlie howled.

The two friends returned to the kitchen. Jane filled the kettle and set it on the stove to boil. She began preparations for baking. A frown creased between her eyebrows. Presently she said: "I wonder if any of the neighbours know the history of this house."

"Maybe some of the really old people do," said Lydia. She settled herself at the table once more and began to chop rhubarb. "What about your friend with the eggs? Hasn't he lived here all his life?"

"He's awfully young to know very much," said Jane. "He's one of the kids I played with when I was little so he's around the same age as I am. I mostly played with him because the other children lived farther away and they weren't as nice as he was." She floured the counter and began to roll out the pastry with Grandma's old rolling pin. "We grew apart as we grew older. He was shy and I guess I must have been too. When the pre-teenage years hit we didn't see one another at all except in passing. Besides, by that time he was doing a man's work on the farm and didn't have time for friends.

"Surely he would've heard the stories as he was growing up."

"I could go see him, I suppose, although I don't

know what his living arrangements are."

"Does it matter?"

"Not really, I guess."

After lunch Jane prepared the chicken and put it into the oven. She added a couple of sticks to the fire and then she and Lydia tidied the kitchen. Jane picked up the basket in which Ian had brought the eggs. "D'you want to come? It'll be a nice walk for Charlie."

Lydia jumped up from her seat by the bay window and grabbed Charlie's leash. "I don't want to stay here by myself, thank you." She hastened out the door ahead of Jane and was half way across the yard before Jane could put away the mop and close and fasten the door.

"This ghost stuff really has you spooked," said Jane when she had caught up to Lydia.

"You bet it has." Lydia stooped to put the leash on Charlie. "I don't know how cousin Gertie does it. She goes out with that ghost hunter every day."

"Is this a job she'd be interested in?"

"I can ask. I'll phone her. I think she should be back by now."

The path across the fields was bordered with daisies and Queen Anne's lace. It traced a red line diagonally across what used to be her grandfather's cow pasture. The rest of the pasture was overgrown with ripening hay and thistles. The edge of the field was surrounded by rusting wire fence, the posts a little askew from age and recent neglect. Jane tugged at the old gate to open it wide enough to slip through. "We'll have to walk around the edge. Ian has this field planted with oats and the path is not there anymore." She turned right and began the trek around the wide field keeping out of the grain. Lydia followed behind holding Charlie's leash firmly. He had caught the scent of a mouse and was determined to follow it. He strained at the leash giving short sharp barks. "C'mon Charlie, cut it out." Lydia shortened the leash so that Charlie had to heel. "You can't hunt mice in Ian's oats." Charlie pulled again despite the shortened leash. "Charlie! Heel! Heel, or it's obedience school for the rest of the summer." Charlie settled briefly until a new scent caught his attention.

"Maybe we should have left him home," said Jane. She pulled at the gate on the other side of the field.

"I don't know what's gotten into him today. He's been to obedience school already."

"New scents, I suppose." Jane pulled the gate shut behind them. "I wonder if we can cross this field or do we have to go around. It looks to be potatoes."

Jane stood for a moment admiring the straight hills of potatoes going over the hill. They were already past flowering. She bent and lifted some leaves. "These will soon be ready for harvest. I remember picking potatoes for Grandpa when I was little. The digger would go down the row and unearth them and we'd follow behind and put them in these big baskets. I could slide it along the ground until it was full but I couldn't lift mine when it was full so someone always had to empty it for me. Now it's all automated."

"Maybe we'd better go around," said Lydia. "I'd hate to spoil the perfection and dear knows what Charlie'll do."

"I guess you're right. I'll ask Ian before we go back."

The three of them trudged around the potato field and out the gate at the other end. "This'll be Ian's back lane," said Jane. "It'll be easier walking now."

"Mm, smell the spruce." Lydia drew in a deep breath of the sweet air. "What is that overlying scent? It smells like perfume." She sniffed again.

Jane sniffed too. "It's ferns. They're all along the fence. And listen ... There's the whine of a locust in the trees." She stood still and listened.

Lydia stood still too. "At least we'll never go hungry." She chuckled. "You know, locusts and wild honey. Look at all those bees."

Jane looked across the fields. The hay field they were passing had lots of wild flowers mixed in and the wild roses along the fence perfumed the air with their sweetness. It was a long, warm walk around the edge of the field and Charlie sat down in the shade of a spruce tree to rest, his red tongue lolling. Jane and Lydia sat down beside him.

"Y'know we're almost there," said Jane. She stretched her slender limbs and luxuriated in the softness of the shed spruce needles. "We'll rest a moment. I wish I'd thought to bring some water with me."

"So does Charlie," said Lydia. She lifted her face to the sun dappling through the tree branches. She closed her eyes and breathed in the fragrance of the spruce tree and the ferns. Charlie rolled over on his side with a doggie sigh and licked his chops.

"We shouldn't stay here too long," said Jane. "It's lovely, but this is a goal-oriented walk and Charlie needs a drink."

Lydia sighed. "Don't we all." She rolled onto her knees and then to her feet. "C'mon, Charlie, Aunt Jane says it's time to go."

Charlie whined and got to his feet.

Jane rose and led the rest of the way to the barnyard gate. "This must be Ian's apple orchard. His father always had the best apples when we were kids. I do remember playing in here. It'll be a little cooler under the trees."

"It's too early for apples yet, I suppose," said Lydia. She pulled the gate wide enough for Charlie to squeeze through then tried to follow. The fit was tight.

Jane watched, then chuckled and finally said: "You have to lift the gate clear of the grass. It's all tangled." She demonstrated. "There used to be a pole gate here and we could just climb through." She walked through the wider opening and pulled it shut behind herself.

"You don't sound as if you knew Ian well when you were young," said Lydia.

"Well enough. I played with him and a couple of others a few times, otherwise I only saw him from a distance. We were never here except for a few weeks at a time. In those days school would be in session all summer because the children had to be on hand for planting in the spring and for picking potatoes in the fall. They'd have time off then. But they had to work just as hard as their parents, so they never got to play with me much. So I just tagged along and picked potatoes." Jane pulled a piece of long grass and stuck it in her mouth.

"Wow! It seems a hard life for children."

"It wasn't easy, but they learned a lot about farming that way. When they were grown they could run the farm almost as well as their parents. A lot of the children would go to Nova Scotia to the agricultural college in Truro for further education after high school." Jane chuckled. "They'd come back with all the latest ideas in farming and try to persuade the old folks how to run things better. Of course, their parents would still be farming. I expect there were a lot of 'discussions' around the kitchen table at night, about how to do things."

"Would anyone get angry enough to just leave home and try their fortunes elsewhere?"

"I suppose so, but I don't think Ian ever did. At least I never heard of it. I had the impression his father was fairly progressive." Jane looked up into the branches of the apple trees. "There's your answer about the apples."

Lydia followed Jane's gaze. "I guess it'll be a few weeks yet."

"Yeah, you'd get the green apple two step from those."

Presently they emerged in Ian's dooryard. Charlie came to a sudden halt at Lydia's feet and sat down. "What's the matter, Charlie? Surely there aren't any ghosties here." Charlie whined.

"I see what his problem is," said Jane. "Ian's dog is just over there." She pointed to the shade of the porch where a black and white bulldog was braced and growling. He crept slowly forward and barked sharply, then continued to growl. Charlie whined and lowered his head. The tip of his tail wagged.

"I'm glad I brought along a doggie treat,"said Jane. She reached into her pocket and pulled out one of Charlie's treats. She held it out to the other dog. "C'mere, boy, this is for you." She took a careful step forward and held the treat. She closed the gap between herself and the dog and gave him the Greenie. The dog sniffed her fingers then began chewing on the bone-shaped treat. "Where's Ian?" she asked when the treat was consumed. "Go find Ian."

The dog alerted at the sound of Ian's name. He allowed Jane to rub his ears. "Find Ian." The dog ran off toward one of the outbuildings.

"He must be over there. We'll wait and see if he comes out."

They watched the dog disappear into the open door of the building and presently Ian came out. He was wiping his hands on an oily rag as he came toward them. "Hello, Jane." He smiled down at her and ignored Lydia for the moment. "What brings you here?"

"I wanted to ask you if you knew anything about Grandma's house." Jane looked up at him, caught up in his blue gaze. She shook her head to straighten her thoughts, then turned to Lydia and Charlie. She cleared her throat "This is my friend, Lydia, and her dog Charlie. They're staying with me for the summer."

Ian turned toward Lydia and held out his hand in greeting. "This is Cedric. He thinks he owns the place."

"That's a good thing," said Lydia. "Charlie's afraid of his own shadow." She watched as Charlie bowed submissively to Cedric's inspection of him.

"Does he bark?" asked Ian.

Jane chuckled. "He barks and howls, but from a distance."

"You'd better come in. I don't see a car so you must have walked over." Ian led the way through the back porch. "You'll probably be thirsty."

"A little," said Lydia. "I don't suppose you could give Charlie a bowl of water."

"Of course," said Ian. He filled a bowl and set it on the floor by the stove. "Tea for you ladies?"

"That'll be very welcome." Jane settled herself in the rocking chair by the hall door. "We haven't picked up the modern habit of carrying our water with us."

Lydia perched on the side of the lounge. "It's just one more thing to carry and I usually have my hands full with Charlie."

Ian filled the kettle from the tap and set it over the firebox to heat. It immediately started to popple and sing.

"You must have just eaten," said Jane. "Your kettle is already singing."

"I keep a stick of wood in there summer and winter. More in the winter. In the summer it's not for warmth for the house, it's just to keep the water tank warm. Your grandpa was smart when he put a water tank in the cellar for your grandma years ago. He was quite inventive and he figured out how to heat it electrically. At the time it was the marvel of the neighbourhood but now everyone has one made commercially. Dad should have followed in his footsteps. Maybe I will yet. It's kind of a nuisance dragging water all the time just to keep the tank filled."

Jane sat pondering the value of having a water tank to fill then realized that she didn't even know where the well was on the farm. She frowned. I wonder if Ian would know, she thought.

"So what brings you ladies out this afternoon?" Ian warmed the teapot with a scoop of water from the stove tank then poured it into the sink and began filling a large tea ball with loose tea.

"We were wondering if you know the history of Grandpa's house."

"Some of it, I guess, although I don't know how accurate it is. It's just what the old folks were willing to talk about."

Ian pulled a chair out from the table and sat

down, the teapot still in his hands. "I heard once that when your Pa and Ma were young they travelled with a somewhat fast crowd, but then his Pa died and left the farm to him on condition that he looked after his Ma for the rest of his life."

"That must have been 'Old Grandma' that my mother talked about. She was quite young when Old Grandma died but she remembered the funeral. They still kept the corpse in the parlour until the funeral."

A grunt of distaste emanated from Lydia.

Ian laughed. "Your friend doesn't like the idea."

"You've never heard of that, Lydia?" asked Jane.

Lydia shook her head and shuddered slightly.

"Yeah," said Jane, "they'd pull the blinds and put a big tub of ice by the casket and close the parlour door to keep the cold in until the funeral. In the winter time they'd store the corpse in an outdoor vault at the cemetery until the ground thawed in the spring and they could dig a grave. You never knew who you'd end up lying beside."

Lydia shuddered again. "Gross!"

The kettle came to a full boil and Ian looked down at the teapot in his hands. "I guess I'd better put the tea down." He rose and carried the teapot to the stove then turned to Jane. "I guess your grandpa did some rum running during prohibition too." He went back to preparing tea and set it to the back of the stove to steep. He turned again toward Jane. "Someone once said that he made a little on the side too until the Mounties shut him down. They never did find his still though, so that may not be true."

"Goodness," said Jane, "I just knew that he raised a few foxes. He used to take me out to see the kits when I was tiny. He warned me not to stick my fingers in the cages. He told me that the Momma fox would bite them off."

"Maybe not off without a little work but she sure could give a nasty bite."

"I could see their sharp little teeth so I never did try it. It's a shame that the fox industry is gone, but I always felt sorry for the foxes."

"Yeah, it was only the fur they were after. I think they sold it for coats for the up and coming people in Europe. I read somewhere that most of the fur went to buyers overseas. It was certainly beautiful enough. I think most of the rest of the animal went for dog meat. It built a lot of fortunes in the early days, and certainly no one from here could have afforded one, never mind have somewhere to wear it." Ian got three mugs down from the cupboard. He checked them for dust then set them on the table. "I don't have much company these days. Everyone's so busy, I have to make an appointment. No one just drops in anymore."

"It's a shame," said Jane. "I know Grandma and

Grandpa always had a lot of company especially on the weekend." She lapsed into silence thinking about how many people she'd met at her Grandmother's table over the years. Then she said: "They seemed to know everyone who was worth knowing in Charlottetown and then some. I've even met people from other countries there."

"I think your grandma moved in theatrical circles when she was young and that's why she knew so many people from abroad. She wasn't from here, you know." Ian rose to pour the tea.

"Didn't she used to sing to us?" asked Lydia. "I seem to remember her singing a lot that time I stayed here when we were in high school. I thought she had a beautiful voice."

Jane frowned trying to remember. "I guess she did. She always seemed to be singing when I was little and she was always sort of a leader in the church choir. I heard Grandpa call her by a funny name once. I asked her about it but she kind of passed it off as a nickname."

Lydia chuckled. "Maybe it was a stage name."

"Ian, you said she wasn't from here," said Jane. "I didn't know that. D'you know where she was from?"

"I think I heard Toronto once, but I can't be sure," said Ian. He thought for a moment then shook his head. "I just don't know. Kids never know."

"Only because adults won't talk," said Jane.

"Some of the things they keep secret are just plain silly when we hear about them later," said Lydia. "Most of their secrets aren't worth keeping."

"And a lot of it was gossip that shouldn't have been spoken of in the first place," said Ian. He picked up the tea pot, lifted the lid and peered inside. "There's a few drops left, shall I make some more?"

"No, we have to get back," said Jane. "I put a chicken in the oven before we left, I want to make sure it actually warmed. It was just the remnants of the morning fire from when I baked the pie. It could still be stone cold."

Chapter Three

Jane stuck a fork in the chicken. "It's a good thing we came back when we did. This is still only half done." She closed the oven door, added a couple of sticks of wood to the dwindling fire then stirred up the ashes. A tiny flame sprang to life. "Supper will be late unless you want to eat out."

"Not really," said Lydia. She tucked her feet under herself in the wing chair opposite the rocker. "I've been looking forward to your chicken all afternoon."

"What's your favourite meal?"

"Macaroni, cheese, broccoli and ham cubes."

"What's so special about that?" Jane clattered the stove lid into place then sat down in the rocker.

Lydia waved her hand. "It was my favourite way to eat broccoli when I was a kid, and you make it just like Mom used to."

"Well, thank you. Your mom was only an okay cook as I remember." Jane looked across the yard to where they had tethered Charlie. He was asleep in the late afternoon sunshine.

"What do you think about what Ian had to say

about your grandmother?" asked Lydia. "Does any of it ring a bell?"

"Faintly. I was too little and it was all so long ago that it's hard to distinguish reality from daydreams. I just remember Grandma singing and wished I could sing like her. You have to remember that we were mainly here during the summer months and school holidays."

"I wonder if she left anything in the attic that could give us a clue?" Lydia stretched her legs out from their cramped position.

"I've never been up there. As children we weren't allowed to go there and we certainly were not allowed to rummage around in her possessions. I've been putting off the job of clearing the attic. I still feel like I shouldn't go up."

"Even after all these years?"

Jane nodded. "Grandma could be quite formidable. She could put the fear into anyone who dared to go against her. It kind of stays with you." Jane pondered all that Ian had said and speculated on. "Now Grandpa, I can imagine him doing all the things Ian said he was rumoured to do. He had a twinkle in his eye when he was about to pull a fast one on Grandma."

"Even bootlegging and rum running?"

"Yeah, I can see him doing that. He was pretty cagey and I'm not surprised that the Mounties couldn't find his still. I doubt even Grandma knew where it was when he was running a batch."

"Hm," said Lydia, "want to go looking tomorrow?"

"No, I do not. It's probably rusted into the ground by now and buried under piles of brush and fallen trees, even if you could get through the undergrowth anymore."

Lydia's eyes sparkled at the idea of an adventure. "I don't believe that copper rusts and we could just take a walk."

"I don't think so." Jane stood up and went to check the chicken. "I'm having enough trouble convincing myself to go up to the attic. I feel guilty just thinking about it." Jane's brow furrowed. "Dear knows what we'll find."

That night Jane was startled awake to the sound of the branches tapping on the side of the house by the head of her bed. I must get someone to trim those off, she thought on the edge of her dream. She opened her eyes to peer at her bedside clock then gasped at the hint of lightness at the foot of her bed. When it had fully gathered, it had the shape of an old woman and it was looking directly at her. It slowly began to dissipate as Jane pulled the covers over her head. The quilt seemed to move at her feet. "It won't do any good, you know," sounded in her ear.

After her heart had slowed to almost normal she peeked out from under the suffocation of the bed covers to see what time it was now. How long had she been under there? A full half hour! Did I fall asleep and just have a nightmare? she wondered. She reached to turn on the light. It's always better with the light on when you're scared, she thought. That's what Mom used to say.

In the kitchen Charlie howled.

"Did you hear Charlie howl last night?" Jane stirred the porridge and watched Lydia out of the corner of her eye.

Lydia yawned and stretched. "I died last night. Didn't hear a thing." She glanced across at Charlie who was lying in the alcove with his snout underneath his paws. He looked thoroughly defeated as only a dog can. "What's the matter with you? Did you have an accident? D'you want to go out?"

The tip of Charlie's tail wagged but his snout remained buried in his paws.

"Walkies?" Lydia rose to get his leash. Charlie rushed to the door. "You're eager." She snapped the leash onto his collar. "Let's go." She slid her bare feet into her old sneakers as Charlie pulled her out the door.

"Don't be long," said Jane. The apprehension engendered by her night time visitor still fluttered in her stomach.

"I may be, if Charlie doesn't slow down. Charlie, remember this is an island. It has edges. You don't want to fall off." The door slammed behind her.

From the parlour a faint chuckle seemed to float on the air. Jane went and closed the door to the parlour and then the door to the kitchen.

Jane pondered the events of last night as she stirred the porridge then set it aside to let it rest. I still can't decide if that was a dream, she thought. She gave herself a little shake and began setting the table. I must see if I can trim those branches back myself. It'll mean getting the ladder up in the first place. I wonder, if it wasn't a dream, who the old lady was. I'd recognize Grandma, so it wasn't her.

On the air, a soft chuckle sounded from the parlour although the doors were closed and the word 'fur' imprinted itself in Jane's mind. She frowned and stood listening, the silverware forgotten in her hand. The sound did not come again. Jane gave herself a mental shake and distributed the silverware.

Lydia clattered into the kitchen, the wooden screen door slapping shut behind her. "I tethered Charlie under the tree. He is spooked this morning. He didn't stop running until we reached the road and then I had to drag him back. I carried him part of the way and he refused to come into the house again."

"I wonder what's got into him?" said Jane.

"It's not at all like him." Lydia dropped into the wing chair and tucked her feet under her to rest and catch her breath.

"And you didn't hear him howl last night about twenty after three?"

"Not a sound. I slept like a log last night. It must have been the walk to Ian's and back that did it. Why?"

Jane recounted the events of the night. It was as if she were back there under the suffocation of the blankets and she began to perspire. "Did I dream it? Was it real?"

"Goodness, Jane, you're as pale as a ghost yourself and sweating like a lumberjack." Lydia sat upright in her chair staring at Jane. "It was real enough to you, that's for sure." She rose from her seat and handed Jane the kitchen towel.

Jane mopped her face. "I thought it was the tree branches scraping the house that woke me but that vision was there when I opened my eyes to look at the clock. Then Charlie howled. I nearly hit the ceiling. Is he as sensitive as all that?" Jane's face had taken on lines of worry.

"And why didn't I hear Charlie? After all, he is my dog." Lydia uncurled her legs. "If it was the tree branches that disturbed you, we need to get them trimmed. It will at least eliminate one of the reasons for uneasy sleep."

"I wonder if you and I can trim those branches ourselves? The ladder's pretty heavy."

Lydia pondered the idea for a moment. "It can't hurt to try."

"As long as we don't fall off."

"We could always ask Ian to do it for us." Lydia's eyes twinkled at Jane.

"Don't match-make," said Jane. She frowned. "He has his own work to do, and besides I don't want to have to tell him about the strange events here. He might think we were going cuckoo."

Lydia laughed. "You were the only one seeing things last night."

Jane and Lydia managed to wrestle the heavy wooden ladder into place. It had taken awhile to find it. "Grandpa must have been very strong to have carried this thing any distance," said Jane. She sat down on the grass to catch her breath.

Lydia plopped down beside her. "It's a long way up from here. Are you sure you want to go up? That ladder is so heavy, that I doubt I could hold it if it did start to slide, and I'm afraid of heights so I'm not leaving the ground."

Jane sighed. "Maybe we should ask Ian. He'll probably laugh at us thinking we could do this."

"It's better to get laughed at than to break our necks," said Lydia.

Jane looked at the ladder and the distance between the top rungs and the ground. "I don't want Ian to break his neck either."

"Thanks," said Ian from the corner of the house. He was carrying a basket of eggs. "I brought these. I thought you could use them."

Jane and Lydia jumped to their feet. "I didn't hear you coming," said Jane.

"I just got here. What are you two trying to do, anyway?"

"Trim the branches," said Lydia.

"We got the ladder here and put it up. It's heavy," said Jane. "We were just catching our breath and deciding if we should try it. I've never trimmed a tree before."

"And I get queasy when I'm off the ground," said Lydia.

Ian pursed his lips in an effort not to smile. His blue eyes twinkled and gave him away. "And you were debating whether your necks were more important than mine."

"You're laughing at us," said Lydia.

His pursed lips widened into a grin. "It's better to be laughed at than to break your necks."

"You heard us! How long were you standing there anyway?" asked Jane.

Ian tested the ladder. "Long enough. Hand me the trimmers and move out of the way of falling debris." He handed the basket of eggs to Lydia. "Mind the eggs." He turned toward the ladder and began steadily climbing. His sturdy frame was soon at the level of the offending branches and he began lopping them off. Fir branches fell like rain and he was soon finished and back on the ground. Lydia and Jane began gathering up the fallen branches.

"Is that everything?" asked Ian. He was looking a little damp around the edges of his curly, red-brown hair. "I can take a look around and see if there's any more trimming to be done."

"Would you? It'll be a great help," said Jane.

Ian was back in a few minutes. "Everything looks ship-shape to me."

"Perfect," said Jane. "Thanks." She began dragging fir cuttings toward the barn.

"Your grandfather had a wheelbarrow, you know." Ian gathered up another armload of twigs and followed Jane behind the barn.

Jane deposited her armload beside the remains of the woodpile. "Where can I get a load of wood for the winter?"

"Jack Murphy sells wood. He's over in Mount Stewart."

Jane frowned. "Where in Mount Stewart?"

"You know where the gas station is by the bridge? Turn there and go across the bridge and at Sam's corner turn right. He's down there about a mile or so."

Jane closed her eyes trying to picture the route. "Sam's corner? I've never heard of it."

"It was the old general store. It burned down before my time but everybody knows where it was."

Jane laughed and shook her head. "Typical Island directions! Someone stopped me on the street once asking where Queen's Arms was. I tried to explain to no avail since the tavern it's named for isn't there anymore either. The poor guy just looked bewildered and moved on."

"Must have been an off-islander."

The clouds began to gather mid-morning and soon a light rain began to fall.

"D'you know, we need groceries," said Jane that afternoon. "The cupboard is almost bare."

"Can we go after supper?" Lydia looked up from the book she was reading.

"If you don't mind going out in the rain to pick lettuce, we can have a chicken salad for supper. I can make a batch of biscuits to go with it. I was going to make cookies anyway."

"Sounds good to me." Lydia went back to her book.

"I thought I might bring some to Ian to thank him for helping us today." Jane clattered in the cupboard getting out the baking sheets. "We can drop them on our way to town."

"Good plan," said Lydia absently.

Soon the kitchen was filled with the familiar smell of spices and baking. Jane savoured the aroma. "Reminds me of Grandma," said Jane.

Lydia grunted an acknowledgement and went on with her reading.

An hour later there was an abundance of cookies and biscuits cooling on racks.

Lydia closed her book with a snap. "You're all done?"

Jane pulled out a kitchen chair and sat down. "You were so taken with your book you never looked up."

"I'm rereading a Jane Austen. I read them over and over when I was little and I wondered if it would still have the same charm for me now, and it does."

"There are more like it in the library. Grandma always had a good selection of books that kids could read and some they shouldn't. I got into *Gone With the Wind* at a very young age. My mother was horrified, but by the time she found out, I had finished all but the last few pages, and she couldn't do any-thing about it then."

Lydia laughed. "I can just imagine it. Your mother was so up-tight."

"Anyway, help yourself to the reading material. Grandpa even had a few racier books hidden behind the others as I found out one day. They were whisked out of my hands immediately, and I got a scolding for looking at such books. I think Grandma must have had a word with Grandpa about it because they disappeared altogether and I haven't seen them since."

"So your Grandma was up-tight too?"

"Not like my mother, but she had very definite ideas on what was suitable for children."

Lydia rose from her seat. "There's a break in the rain. I'd better go get that lettuce now if I don't want to get soaked."

Jane handed her a bowl. "Wear your rubbers. It's muddy out there."

It was late dusk when Jane and Lydia returned from town. As they drove up the lane they could hear Charlie howling. "He's practically beside himself," said Lydia, "I wonder what's wrong?"

Jane avoided another pothole. "He's probably just lonely."

"But we couldn't take him with us. It's warm enough already that we couldn't leave him in the car."

They rounded the last corner in the lane and emerged from the fir-lined darkness. The house was ablaze with light. Every light in the house was on. "I didn't leave lights on, did you?" asked Jane. She stopped in the middle of the yard and stared at the house. In the yard Charlie danced and pulled at his tether trying to escape into the darkness of the spruce grove. "Whatever is going on in there?"

Lydia pulled her knees up to her chest and hugged them tightly as if she could protect herself from whatever was in the house. "I don't know," she whispered. "I don't like to think about it so I don't." Her voice trembled. "I don't want to find out either." She sounded as if she were about to cry.

"I'll get Charlie and put him in the back seat." Jane climbed out of the car and opened the back door for the dog. Then went over to Charlie with his leash and clipped it on his collar before releasing him from his tether. She led him to the car and encouraged him inside. "The poor beast is trembling." Charlie buried his face in his paws and whined.

"So'm I," said Lydia. She reached back to stroke Charlie's silky ears.

Jane got back in and slammed the door. "I

thought you were going to call cousin Gertie."

"I did but they've been away for the last week or so. Her husband had a psychology convention out west and they decided to take the children and make a vacation of it. And you'd better not call her Gertie to her face either. She hates that name. She says Gertrude is bad enough."

"Well, try her again," said Jane. "This can't go on. If we don't get to the bottom of this I won't be able to live in the house."

"I think we should go and get Ian. He can go in with us and check the house and we can turn out the lights."

"He'll think we're nuts." Jane continued to stare at the lights streaming from the windows. "There doesn't seem to be any movement in there. I'm going in." She reached for the door handle just as Charlie howled again. Jane startled. "This is non-sense. I'm going into my own house and whoever's in there can like it or lump it, I don't care." She strode across the yard and inserted her key in the lock. It wouldn't turn. "What?!" She tried again. From the car she could hear Charlie howling. "Okay, ghost, whoever you are, this is it. I'm not putting up with this anymore," she muttered and tried the lock again. It still would not budge. Jane ran to the car.

"I guess we'll have to get Ian to help us. I can't get the door unlocked." She slammed the door with one hand and started the engine with the other at the same time, then headed down the lane in a spray of gravel. "I hope he doesn't laugh at us."

"He does have a sense of humour," said Lydia. She uncurled from her fetal position and hung on to the ceiling handle for safety as Jane careened around potholes and occasionally bounced in and out of one to the detriment of her undercarriage. "I saw him trying not to laugh at us trying to trim trees the other day."

"It was kind of funny," agreed Jane. She took the corner onto the road, skidding a little on the turn. "A couple of old maids like us trying to do a man's work when we could hardly lift the ladder, and you afraid of heights besides."

The drive to Ian's was fast and silent. Fortunately this quiet road through the woods was fairly well-maintained and they didn't meet any oncoming traffic. Jane slid to a halt in Ian's dooryard and scrambled out. She ran up the steps to the porch and pounded on the door.

Ian switched on the yard light and peered out the door. "Jane! Whatever is the matter? You're as white as a sheet."

"You should see Lydia," said Jane. "And Charlie's in the back seat with his head buried in his paws."

She drew a deep breath to calm her nerves and tumbled the story out to Ian. "I hope you don't think we're out of our minds. But we need your help. Someone's in the house and turned all the lights on and locked the door and we can't get in and I don't even know if I want to go in and, and ... I just so hope you don't think we're crazy, but I'm pretty sure we have at least one ghost." She stopped talking abruptly and stood staring at Ian. Her eyes filled with tears.

Ian pulled her into his arms in a comforting hug. "I'm glad you came," he said. "Just let me get my jacket on and I'll go right over." He grabbed his tattered old barn jacket from the hook behind the door and picked up his baseball bat from the corner where it stood as a deterrent to possible intruders. "I'll go ahead." He slammed the door behind himself and headed for his truck whistling for Cedric on the way.

The return trip was more reasonable safety-wise than the trip over. The lights still blazed brightly from the windows. Even the attic windows were alight. There was no sound and no apparent movement inside. Ian stood and surveyed the situation. "There doesn't seem to be anything going on in there." He frowned. "I'm going in. I know the pantry window is always unlocked so unless one of you or the ghost locked it, I can get in that way.

C'mon, Cedric!" Ian shouldered his baseball bat and headed for the side of the house. He soon had the porch door open from the inside. "These rooms are clear," he called across the yard just as all the lights went out at once. "Dang!" said Ian. "Where do you keep your flashlights?"

Jane edged closer to the door. "First drawer by the door." She stopped in the doorway. "Try the light switch, Maybe the problem's electrical." Ian flipped the switch in the kitchen and the light came on restoring some sense of security to the homey room.

"I'll take the flashlight with me anyway, just in case." He picked up his bat in one hand and the flashlight in the other. "I'll just check the fuse box first." He strode across the porch and opened the fuse box door. He went down the row of fuses and shook his head. "This is hopelessly out of date. It's a wonder you haven't had problems. Did you contact the electrician like you said you would?"

Jane nodded. "He said he'd come by next week but that was two weeks ago."

"Who'd you call?"

Jane told him.

Ian clucked his tongue. "That fellow won't be here until Christmas."

"What am I to do in the meantime?"

"You didn't sign any contracts with him, did you?"

"No. I only talked to him on the phone. He said he'd be down the next day, but he didn't show and then he called and said he'd be down next week, and then the next week it was the same thing and he still hasn't showed."

"Wish you'd asked me. He's unreliable that way. He has a reputation although I didn't know it was this bad. I'll call my buddy, George. He'll likely make time to come tomorrow if I ask him."

Jane visibly relaxed. Some colour was returning to her cheeks.

"There's nothing wrong here so let's see about the rest of the house." He closed the fuse box door and headed toward the kitchen. "I'm going to see if the bulbs are hot in the lamps before I turn them on." He went room by room through the whole house with Jane close behind. At the hall door Cedric whined his distress at having to pass the parlour door and refused to leave the kitchen.

"That's odd," said Ian. "Cedric's usually obedient. Why did he baulk here?"

"I don't know," Jane replied, "but Charlie does the same thing."

"Hm," Ian pursed his lips. "That is odd." He peered around the corner of the door into the parlour. "Does that rocking chair always rock like that?"

"Not always, just sometimes. It was glowing one night."

Ian crept toward the rocker and put out his hand to stop it. He pulled his hand back quickly as if stung. "Ow! I just got a shock off the thing."

The rocking chair continued to rock more vigorously now and an eerie chuckle filled the room.

"That happens all the time too," said Jane. "It doesn't seem to matter whether it's day or night."

"I think you really might have ghosts," said Ian.

"I don't believe in ghosts!" Jane stamped her foot like a child.

"I don't either, but I think I'll have to change my mind." He slipped his hand under the lampshade to see if the bulb was hot. It was old and incandescent and definitely warm to the touch. "This has been on recently. Let's see if the other ones are hot too."

Every light bulb in the house was warm and every light in the house worked. They returned to the kitchen. Ian sat down at the table and leaned his chin in his hand. "D'you want me to stay here tonight? I could sleep on the lounge."

Jane picked up the kettle and began filling it while she thought over Ian's offer. "I would, but if I have to live with ghosts I'd better get used to it."

"By the way, where are Lydia and Charlie?"

"She's outside trying to coax Charlie out of the back seat. Besides, I don't think think she's very brave about such adventures as ghosts. I'm not sure she'll even want to stay here anymore. We haven't discussed it."

"You'll be here by yourself then," said Ian. "Won't that be a little unnerving for you?"

Jane shrugged one shoulder. "Like I said, if I have to live with ghosts, I might as well get used to it. Lydia's cousin works with that ghost buster guy out in Cherry Valley but Lydia said she's away on vacation just now."

"Can they really bust ghosts?"

Jane set the kettle on the stove to heat. "Lydia says they can. I wouldn't know."

The back door slammed and Lydia came into the kitchen. She was sweating and flushed and thoroughly flustered.

"What's the matter Lydia? You look distressed," said Jane.

"I am distressed," grumbled Lydia. "That Charlie can be one stubborn dog. I could not get him out of the back seat. He wouldn't be coaxed out, I couldn't threaten him out and he was determined that I wasn't going to push him out. He all but snapped at me at which point I picked him up bodily, carried him out and slammed the door so he couldn't get back in. He's one heavy dog." She flopped into the rocker, leaned her head back and closed her eyes. "I'm tired."

"Where's Charlie now?" asked Jane.

"Tethered under the spruce tree and very

unhappy. He's all hunkered down with his snout buried under his paws, whining." Lydia closed her eyes. "I'll check him later and bring him some fresh water and dog food. He can stay outside for the night."

"What if it rains?" asked Ian.

"That's his own fault. He can just suffer. I'll get him a dog house tomorrow."

"Why don't you lock him in the barn?" said Jane. "It's dry and there's still a lot of hay around, he can make himself comfortable in that."

"Good idea. I'll see to it in a minute." She opened her eyes. "Is that tea I see?"

"It is." said Jane. "I thought we needed a restorative after all the drama." She retrieved three mugs from the cupboard and poured the tea. "It's a shame we don't have any of Grandpa's hooch to put in it. We could all use a wee dram after that."

From the parlour came the sound of laughter. "Did you hear that?" Jane's eyes were wide with fright. She looked from one to the other. They both nodded, their mouths agape, their eyes as wide as Jane's.

Ian strode toward the parlour and stopped short in the doorway. The house suddenly went eerily quiet and there was nothing to be seen, not even the rocking chair moved.

Ian stayed the night as he had suggested. The house, for now, was quiet. Charlie spent the night in the barn under a mound of hay where he had buried himself, all but the end of his nose and the tip of his tail. Cedric was convinced to come into the house and sleep on the floor next to the lounge where Ian slept.

Jane got up before the rooster crowed the next morning. Ian woke as she entered the kitchen. "Good morning, Jane, did you sleep well?" Ian rolled onto his side to watch Jane bustle around the kitchen and make breakfast.

"I did. But more to the point, did you? That lounge is pretty solid to sleep on."

"It is, but I did okay. Cedric was a good doggy too." Cedric wagged his tail and went to scratch at the porch door. Ian rolled to a sitting position and pulled on his trousers. Cedric scratched more vigorously. "Hold your horses, Cedric, I'm coming." Ian stuck his stockinged feet into his shoes and let Cedric out for a run.

"I hope he comes back," said Jane. "He may not after last night's adventures."

"He'll come back. He knows who feeds him." Ian buttoned his shirt and tucked it into his trousers.

"Shall I take Charlie his breakfast?"

"Take his leash and and tether him under the spruce tree before you give it to him though. He'll have to come out of the barn to get his breakfast and you can shut the door behind him."

Lydia wandered into the kitchen and collapsed into the rocking chair rubbing the sleep out of her eyes. "Where's Ian?"

"Out feeding Charlie."

"Good man," said Lydia. "I was not looking forward to wrestling Charlie out of the barn this morning." She yawned and stretched. "Anything I can do to help with breakfast?"

"You can set the table and put the toast in while I tend the bacon." Jane turned back to her task. "I won't do the eggs until Ian gets back."

The screen door slapped shut and Ian came in. "That Charlie, he did not want to come out of the barn at all. I had to find him first: he was buried under about a foot of hay in the back of a stall. Then I had to grab him and carry him out to tether him and give him his breakfast." Ian pulled out a chair from the table and sat down. "He looked at me so sadly and whined when I left him. I didn't have much sympathy for him by that time."

"Is Cedric still out and about?" asked Jane.

"He's still out. I didn't see him. I was too intent on herding Charlie. Cedric may have gone home."

"How d'you like your eggs?"

"Over easy," replied Ian. "And is that bacon I smell?"

"It sure is," said Jane. She broke eggs into the bacon grease then poured the tea. "Lydia, if you will fetch the milk and sugar please." She deftly flipped the eggs without breaking the yolks. "Perfect. Ketchup too, please, Lydia." She ladled eggs onto the plates just as the toast popped.

After breakfast Ian leaned back and patted his stomach. "That was excellent, Jane." He sipped the last of his tea. "So, Lydia, Jane tells me that you have a cousin who knows that ghost buster guy. Maybe it's time to invite her out for a visit."

"We have to do something," said Jane. She poured another cup of tea all around. "There were never such goings on when Grandma was alive and well. Although she did say once that she saw what she thought was a friend of hers in the parlour. She said that this friend had died a few years ago. She said she was sitting in the rocking chair. She never said who it was. I wouldn't have known her anyway. I was just a child."

"I'll try Gertrude again today," said Lydia. "She's been out of town for the last few weeks. She should be home by now, and I agree, we do need to do something. This is getting worse every night."

Gertrude was invited to tea and arrived mid-afternoon. She was a former nurse who had worked at the old folks home. One of her former patients was an old lady called Molly who had since died. Molly now had other-worldly pals, and they had once ganged up on Gertrude to convince her of her mediumship abilities.

Gertrude pulled out a chair at the kitchen table and made herself comfortable. She had let her red curls grow and now wore them in a pile on top of her head. Tendrils of red curls had escaped the brush and lay in ringlets at the base of her neck. "So I hear you have ghosts," she said.

"We have something," said Jane, "and it has been getting worse."

"We're getting tired of being confined to the kitchen of an evening and being wakened in the middle of the night," said Lydia. "And I mean literally tired. We're really not getting much sleep."

Gertrude smiled. "They can be disrupting if they put their minds to it. How long has this been going on?"

"It started when I moved in but before Lydia came, and it has been progressing."

"How does it manifest?" asked Gertrude.

"Chuckles of laughter, rocking chairs that rock by themselves, a glowing figure in the chair. I even had a visitation in my bedroom the other night," said Jane. "The only good thing about all of this is that whoever she is she does dishes." Jane began to laugh but it rose into an almost hysterical shriek. She took a deep breath and caught hold of herself.

"What about the electrical problems and all the lights on and the locked door just the other night?" asked Lydia. "Never mind the muddy footprints on the stairs."

Jane made a face. "All that too."

"And you didn't tell me about the visitations," said Lydia. "The way you told it, I just thought you'd had a bad dream. Besides, I slept like a log that night. Better than I'd slept in ages."

"I didn't want to send you screaming back to Charlottetown." Jane poured tea into mugs and passed the plate of cookies. "Help yourself."

"So it really is getting intrusive." Gertrude helped herself to a second cookie. "I shouldn't really because I gained a little weight on our trip and I can't let it get ahead of me. It's too hard to get off."

"Poor Charlie is terrorized. He won't even come into the kitchen anymore," said Lydia. "He spends his nights in the barn now, buried under a mound of old hay."

"Charlie's your dog? They often sense things that we don't."

"Yeah, I decided to get one to keep some of the relatives at bay."

Gertrude laughed. "You must have had a visitation of a relative kind, eh?"

Lydia made a face. "You could say that. I just hope they don't decide to come next year."

"The way they eat they probably won't make it 'til next year," said Jane.

Lydia sighed. "I don't want them dead, I just want them to rent a hotel room somewhere in Summerside."

"In other words, good and far away." Gertrude drained the last of her tea. "That was a real treat. Thank you, Jane. Now, I need to have a look at the venue." She rose from her chair. "D'you know the history of the house?"

"Not really. I just know it's old. The beams, where you can see them, have been carved with an axe and joined with pegs."

"So it's very old. A couple of hundred years, d'you think?"

Jane shrugged. "Probably. I understand from my mother that Grandpa bought it in the early teens. She didn't know anything else. Of course, she's gone now, so I can't ask her."

"That's fine, we can find out other ways."

Jane turned and led the way down the hall and turned in at the parlour door. "That's the rocking chair that rocks by itself and glows."

"Is this where the chuckles come from?"

Jane nodded. "Everything is still and quiet now, wouldn't you know."

"That's often the way. Spirits know who can reach them and who can't."

"D'you have contacts on the other side?" asked Lydia. Her brow wrinkled in distress.

"I have a person I knew before she died who will talk to me," said Gertrude. "I don't talk about her because most people wouldn't understand. They're usually afraid of psychics and what they can see. Most of them are afraid that I'll go after their darkest secrets. I'm not nosy that way, and it wouldn't be polite either, but they mostly don't believe me. I have to pick my friends carefully."

"It must get lonely," said Jane.

"It can. I stay connected through church and portray myself as a secretary to Jim. He's the guy who is known in some circles as the ghost buster. He lives in Cherry Valley in that house on the corner with all the antennas on the roof. He has a friend, Mary Ann, who helps him with his investigations, and me as well. So no one really knows what I do. I will appreciate it if you keep that bit of information to yourselves."

"Of course," chorused Jane and Lydia.

The tour of the house continued. "What's behind that door?" Gertrude pointed to the attic door.

"I see it's locked."

"It goes to the attic and I don't know where the key is. We were never allowed to play up there when we were children. It was very forbidden. I'm still reluctant to even try the door," said Jane. "Grandma was a fierce old lady when she wanted to be. I didn't dare cross her. I don't think my mother did either."

"I'd like to see up there," said Gertrude. "Will you mind if I bring in a locksmith set?"

Jane sighed. "I suppose not. She's been gone a few months now so what could it matter?" Jane felt the heavy beating of her heart but said nothing. Her grandmother's face with its fierce scowl when she was angry appeared in Jane's consciousness. She shivered but said nothing.

Gertrude noticed. "The old lady's around is she?"

Jane nodded. "I think so. I got a strong memory of her angry face just now."

"When you said I could look in the attic?"

"Yeah. Just about then. I guess she doesn't want us messing with her things even now."

Gertrude reached over and patted Jane's arm reassuringly. "Those old ladies bark worse than they bite. She really can't do anything to you from the other side, you know."

"Logically I know that," said Jane. "How could they? They're there and we're here." Somewhere in the house a door slammed. Everyone startled, even Gertrude. "Wow, she really doesn't like to be crossed."

"She never did. I was scared of her."

"I think this is going to be a very interesting case," said Gertrude. "I'll run it by Jim and see what he thinks about it." Several doors in the house slammed hard enough to shake the structure.

"The sooner the better," said Jane.

CHAPTER FOUR

The phone rang a few days later. Jane answered. "Oh, hello, Gertrude, I was wondering when we'd hear from you."

Gertrude's voice came down the line. "I had to catch up with Jim and Mary Ann first. And then, of course, there's Molly. She was off gallivanting somewhere on the other side with Larry. They've become quite an item these last few years."

"Who's Mary Ann?"

"She's our assistant and Jim's sort of other half. They don't live together but she's just across the field from Jim's. She's a psychic like I am and a good friend. She trained me when I was just starting out. We still do most of our cases together. Jim is not a psychic but he's very committed to increasing the world's knowledge about things ethereal. My husband and he were best friends since high school. Mary Ann taught me most of what I know about being psychic. "

"And who is Molly?"

Gertrude chuckled. "Molly's a character. I don't know if you can actually meet her but she's the one I mentioned the other day. She was a patient of mine a number of years ago at the nursing home where I worked. She subsequently 'died' as they say on this side, but she's very much alive in the so-called afterlife. She helps us from that side. She can access information that we would have no idea even existed and couldn't get to if we did know. She and her friend, Lucy. Molly is quite a character and very feisty. She's also prone to act before she thinks. Lucy was her friend in this life but she died before Molly. Poor Lucy was tasked to keep Molly in some sort of check as best she could. Larry is their boss but he and Molly have become a twosome since she passed. They are rarely apart."

"I see. At least, I think I see."

"You'll get used to it. Looking at it from the usual perspective makes it seem strange at first, but as you come to understand about energy and spirit and all the stuff that goes with it, you'll understand better. Anyway, on to practical matters. Are you free this evening? Jim and Mary Ann have decided to take the case and the sooner we get started, the sooner we clear your house."

"We'll be here. D'you mind if Ian joins us? I don't feel very safe dealing with the ghosts by ourselves after you've gone."

"Ian's a friend?"

"A neighbour and very level-headed. Also what

should we do with the dog, Charlie?"

"Lock him in the barn. If he's on the loose he'd probably run away.

Jane laughed. "Who? Ian or Charlie?"

Gertrude chuckled. "We'll see you this evening about seven."

"I'm so glad you agreed to come over for this event, Ian." Jane began to clear away the plates from supper.

"I wouldn't pass up a home cooked meal." Ian patted his stomach. "That roast was as good as your grandmother used to make, and that's saying something."

"She taught me everything I know about cooking and baking," said Jane. "My own mother couldn't cook very well. She wasn't bad, just not as good as Grandma."

"You learned well. That rhubarb pie was the best I've had for a long, long time."

"It's about time to lock Charlie in the barn," said Lydia. "I can see he's not happy out there in the yard." She rose and lifted Charlie's leash from the hook by the door. "What about Cedric?"

"I left him home 'guarding' the house. There's nothing actually to guard but he doesn't know that. At least I don't think he does. He wasn't happy about being left behind. A ride in the truck holds magical powers for him."

Lydia disappeared outdoors. Ian rose and pulled down the dish towel from the drying rack behind the stove. "I talked to my friend, the electrician. He said he could come out the first of next week. He can't come any sooner because he's putting in a lot of overtime at that new apartment building on the waterfront. You'll just have to hold out until then."

"I can last another few days. If the other fellow can make me wait for weeks what's another few days?"

"Indeed," said Ian. He wiped dishes in silence for a few minutes then said: "Is your friend going to be here with you all summer?"

"Off and on." Jane wrung out her dishcloth and hung it over the spout in the sink to dry. "Why do you ask?"

"No reason, just wondering."

Jane began plumping the cushions on the rockers and the window seat. Ian hung his damp dish towel on the rack behind the stove. Jane looked up just in time to see the wet dishcloth she had hung on the faucet hit Ian in the neck and fall to the floor.

Ian grunted and bent to retrieve the dishcloth. "You didn't need to throw it at me." He hung the dishcloth on the rack. "All you had to do is ask."

"I-I didn't throw it." Jane's eyes were enormous.

"I was over here plumping cushions. I hung it on the spout."

Ian looked at her from the corner of his eye then looked at the dishcloth hanging on the rack. "Well, someone did and you're the only one here."

"I didn't!" Jane regained her breath. "I looked up just in time to see it hit."

"I'm glad your friend's cousin is coming this evening. This is serious."

At the appointed time Gertrude and her friends arrived at the farm. Even Don, Gertrude's husband came, mainly to keep their son, Roddy, out of trouble and tend to the baby. The baby was their second child, and they still hadn't named her. It was a difficult decision, and they were no closer to naming her than they had been when she was born three weeks ago. There was no family name that they cared to pass on. Gertrude was breast feeding, so it was not convenient to leave the baby at home.

After introductions were made, Gertrude put the baby beside the stove in her basket. Jane gave them a tour of the house. Everyone, including Roddy, trailed upstairs, their footsteps noisy on the uncarpeted steps. At the top of the stairs Roddy shrieked and grabbed Gertrude by the thigh and buried his curly head in the folds of her skirt. In the barn Charlie howled. After a moment Roddy gathered his composure and peeked out, then turned and stood staring at the door to the attic.

"Whatever is the matter, Roddy?" Gertrude knelt down to face her son.

His face was stark white in contrast to his red curls so like his mother's. He pointed at the door. "I saw someone. He frightened me."

Jane and Lydia looked at one another. "That door's been locked all my life and I can't find the key. There can't possibly be anyone there." She ran up the six steep steps and tried the door handle. It was still locked.

"Was it a man or a woman you saw?"

"It was a man. I think."

"What did he look like?"

"He was old. He had on a grey sweater. He was looking at me."

"Oh, dear," said Gertrude. "It sounds like a repeat of the events at Amanda's. She was another case I worked on a few years ago." She gave Roddy a hug then looked up at Don. "Why don't you take Roddy out around the door yard and go see Charlie."

"It'll be a relief," said Don. "C'mon Roddy, let's go and meet Charlie before it gets too dark. I'll check the baby before I leave."

"Don't let Charlie out," called Lydia after Don. "He likes to go visiting Cedric." She turned her attention back to the tour.

"So who was Roddy seeing?" asked Jim. "Anyone you know?"

Jane wrinkled her brow. "It sort of sounded like Grandpa. He always wore a grey sweater in the evening, and he was just as adamant as Grandma that the attic was off-limits to children. Did either of you see anything?"

"I wasn't paying attention. I was listening to what you guys were saying. Did you see anything, Mary Ann?"

"Not really. I thought I saw a flash of white just as Roddy screamed. But I could have imagined it."

"We'll trance this area first I think," said Gertrude.

"Not 'til we've had our tea," said Jane.

"Are you nervous about what we'll find?" asked Mary Ann.

Jane took a deep breath. "I think I must be. My stomach has been in a knot all day. I don't know what's going on here. I don't know about psychics or the afterlife or anything else. I just know that I want to be able to sleep at night."

Mary Ann put a plump, motherly arm around Jane's shoulders. "Don't worry, Gertrude and I will get to the bottom of it. Why don't you go and put the kettle on. "

The tour continued throughout the upstairs. Gertrude and Mary Ann asked many questions about the recent events. The summer sunset began to fade, and rather than turn on the lights, Gertrude declared them done, and they went downstairs.

In a few minutes Don and Roddy returned from their rambles. "Look what I found, Mommy. Daddy said it's copper." He held up a short piece of bent and flattened pipe. It had been pounded on one end to render its diameter somewhat smaller than the main pipe. Gertrude examined the pipe then held it in her hands and closed her eyes. "This feels as if it has been in the earth for a number of years. It was part of a fairly large construction." She opened her eyes and looked at Roddy, then at Don. "Where did you find it?"

"Roddy found it behind the barn in the weeds. I think there's more than that out there, but it looks like junk. I don't know how he saw it. It was pretty well hidden." Don's face held worry lines. "It was hot when I picked it up. D'you suppose ... ?"

"How did you find it, Roddy?" asked Gertrude.

"A man showed me," replied Roddy. "Can I have it back? The man said not to lose it."

Gertrude turned to Don. "What man?"

Don shook his head. "None that I could see. Was it the same man that you saw upstairs, Roddy?"

"I think it might have been. It looked like him. He had a sweater on. He wasn't as scary."

"Did the man say why you weren't to lose it?" asked Gertrude.

"He said he might need it again. He was looking for it for a long time." Roddy yawned. "Can I sit on the couch, Mommy? I'm tired."

"You may sit on the lounge," said Gertrude, "but take your shoes off if you're going to lie down." She turned her attention back to the piece of copper piping.

She closed her eyes again and fingered the piece gently. She turned it over and over, feeling it from every side, then raised it up to her nose and sniffed it. The faint odour of ancient rum seemed to emanate from the interior of the pipe. She opened her eyes and blinked in surprise, then sniffed again. "Was your grandfather a still man?"

"D'you mean did he distill rum?" asked Jane. "Rumour has it that he was a rum runner during Prohibition so he could very well have been distilling it too. I wouldn't know. We've never found his still."

"D'you suppose he buried it?" said Jim. He had been silent during the tour and listened intently to Roddy's talk of the man. His bulky frame had been a comfort and defence on other cases. His dark hair had greyed slightly at the temples over the years. He was also noticeably thinner on top though not yet bald. He and Don had been high school buddies but their paths had taken them in very different directions since then, although they had remained friends.

Jane shrugged. "If he had one and wanted to hide it, he could have buried it. He knew everyone around, including the government agents who were looking for stills." She poured mugs of tea and set out the milk and sugar. "I even met a few of them when I was little. Of course, I didn't know why they were here." She set out a tin of molasses cookies. "Does anyone like butter on their cookies?"

Gertrude drained her mug then patted her stomach. "That was good. I haven't had one of those soft molasses cookies since I visited my own grandmother." She looked across at Mary Ann. "Are you ready, partner?"

"I'm ready for just about anything," said Mary Ann.

"We'll need to do this on our own." said Gertrude. "You guys can remain here unless we call you." She rose from her chair. "I think we'll start with the parlour, Mary Ann. What d'you think?"

Mary Ann shrugged a plump shoulder. "Sounds

good to me. From what Jane said, this is where most of the activity occurs, although I would like to get into the attic."

"The ghosties do like attics," agreed Gertrude.

They entered the parlour. Mary Ann looked around herself. One wall was covered with built-in bookcases. The opposite wall had an ornate surround on the chimney that looked larger than the fireplace beneath. The bow window was covered with heavy drapery that had faded in the sun. She pulled the drapes closed then settled herself in the big armchair and kicked off her shoes. "The air feels unsettled in here."

"Mm," said Gertrude. "I think they've already figured out that we're onto them." She sat down in the armchair across from Mary Ann and pulled the afghan around herself. She leaned back and eased her shoulders into the cushiony depths. "They sure knew how to make armchairs back in Grandma's day." She closed her eyes and prepared to trance. "I hope it doesn't get too cold."

Mary Ann followed her into trance.

The scene appeared in their minds as if it were still real. The parlour was as it used to be, only looking a little more unfurnished than it was now. There were fewer books on the shelves and there were no drapes, just sheer curtains and window blinds. A few ornaments stood on tables and shelves, some still in the room now, but in different places. There were no lamps. Where the ornate fireplace surround was in the present day the old brickwork was exposed with a mantel shelf over the fireplace itself. A woman's figure sat in the rocking chair in the bow window watching out the lane. Her hair was tied back in a long braid that was wrapped around her head and her long dress of dark blue velvet reached to the floor. She wore a tiara.

"What do you want?" asked Gertrude.

The vision looked at the two psychics but appeared not to hear.

"What do you want?" asked Gertrude again. "What's your name?"

The vision looked startled and seemed to try to respond. The whispery sound was unintelligible.

"I can't hear you," said Gertrude. "Tell me your name again, a little louder if you can."

The vision seemed to take a deep breath before saying: "My name is Julia."

"Thank you," said Gertrude. "That was much better. Is there something we can do for you?"

"Find my coat." The sentence was whispery and faint.

The vision began to fade.

"Don't go, Julia," said Gertrude. "We'd really like to talk to you." But Julia had vanished.

Gertrude came out of trance. "Drat! I was so

hoping to get more information than that."

Mary Ann sat up in the rocking chair and looked across at Gertrude with bright blue eyes. "My attention faded and I couldn't give her any more energy. I'm sorry we lost her."

"At least we know her name now," said Gertrude. "Maybe Jane will know who she is. Shall we try again?"

Mary Ann nodded then closed her eyes. After a few minutes they both opened their eyes again. "What's the matter with us?" she asked. "I can't seem to hold my concentration long enough to see anything tonight."

"Perhaps you're tired," said Gertrude. "I know I've had a long day with the children and I didn't have time for a nap this afternoon."

"I read all afternoon," said Mary Ann.

"Heavy reading?"

Mary Ann grinned. "The book was heavy." She grew serious. "It was heavy reading. It was a book by Annie Besant. She was a big deal in the spiritualist movement in the 19th century. She had some very interesting ideas. I've been trying to get it on inter-library loan for weeks now, but I finally found a copy when I was over to Moncton last week at that used bookstore on the square. I snatched it up despite the price."

"So the wording was Victorian never mind the

subject matter and how dense it was," said Gertrude.

Mary Ann stretched and yawned. "You can borrow it after I've read it if you want."

"I guess we'd better call it a night, then. We can start fresh tomorrow evening. Maybe try the attic."

"At least we got her name."

In the kitchen Don was trying to pacify a crying infant with teaspoonsful of warm milk to no avail. "You guys weren't long." He thrust the squalling baby into Gertrude's arms. "She doesn't like cow's milk."

"I know, and I forgot to pack any pumped milk, never mind a bottle of formula," said Gertrude "She doesn't like that much either but at least she'll drink it." She sat down in the rocker and pulled a blanket over herself and the baby and prepared to suckle the infant. Silence was restored in the kitchen. "To answer you, no, we weren't long. We lost energy too soon. But we did get a name." She began to croon to the baby.

Everyone turned to Mary Ann. "So what was the name?" asked Jane.

"Did your grandmother know a person called Julia?"

Jane blinked and thought hard. "I didn't know all her friends. She had a best friend called Ingrid from her opera days. I believe she kept in touch with her some. I think she's dead now though."

"She'd be pretty old if she's still alive," said Jim. "I wonder if the archives could tell us something?"

"I think she died before Grandma. I think I remember something about that from when I was about ten or so. I don't know. It's all so long ago."

Gertrude looked up from her motherly duty and adjusted her clothing. "If you could get a locksmith to attend to the attic door in the next few days we might find something in the attic that'll tell us who Julia is."

"Did your grandma keep a diary?" asked Mary Ann.

"I don't know that either," said Jane. "It wasn't among her things when I cleared out the house. Perhaps in the attic."

"All the more reason to get a locksmith," said Jim. He dandled Roddy on his crossed leg until Roddy giggled. "Jimmy Gaudet has a business, I think."

"Can you call him in the morning?" asked Jane. "Will you have time?"

"I can call him," said Mary Ann. "He did some work for me when I first moved in at Cherry Valley."

Sunshine and scudding clouds brightened the farmyard the next morning. Chickadees sang in the spruces beside the lane. Starlings and blue jays fought over the seed in the bird feeder, and sparrows and Juncos pecked at the fallen seed. Lydia made her way across the yard to release Charlie from the barn. She found him under a pile of straw.

"C'mon Charlie, time for breakfast. It's a glorious morning and there's work to be done."

Charlie wuffed, then sneezed as he crawled out of his bed.

Lydia set off for the house then realized that Charlie wasn't following. She looked back. He was sitting on the stone step of the barn looking as forlorn as only Charlie could look.

"C'mon, Charlie, brekkies," called Lydia. She stood looking back at Charlie.

Charlie whined and lay down resting his head on his fore paws, barely moving his eyebrows as he watched Lydia make her way toward him.

"What's the matter, Charlie?" She leaned over to scratch Charlie's tawny ears.

Charlie whined again but did not move.

Lydia grabbed him by the collar. "For goodness sake, Charlie, you're a real washout as a companion and protector. You'll be very hungry if you don't come and get your kibble. I'm not bringing it out here." She picked up Charlie and carried him across the yard. "Oof, you're heavy, Charlie, this mode of transportation is not going to last very long." She carried him into the porch and set him down next to his food bowl. Charlie whimpered and ducked his head. Lydia scooped a bowlful of kibble from the bag and set it front of Charlie. He whined and sniffed at it then nibbled at the top few pieces.

"Would you like it better if I put it outdoors?"

Charlie went to the door and scratched. Lydia picked up the bowl and carried it outside to the shade of the tree. She refilled Charlie's water dish from the outside faucet and set it beside the food dish then turned and went indoors.

"I don't know what's gotten into Charlie today. You'd think he'd be happy to get out of the barn after being shut up all night." Lydia pinched off a piece of dough from the cookie dough that Jane was rolling and popped it into her mouth then wiped her sticky fingers on the kitchen towel.

"Why? What's wrong with him?" Jane continued pushing dough around on the counter top with the rolling pin. Her apron was old-fashioned and faded from many washings. It was one her grandmother had made out of scraps of material from a pair of Grandpa's old pyjamas. She brushed the excess flour from her fingers on it after flouring the counter as she rolled.

"First he wouldn't come out of the barn and then he wouldn't come with me. I had to carry him across the yard. I got him in the porch and he wouldn't eat and he couldn't wait to get outside. I've got him tethered under the tree with his bowls."

"I wonder if he's still distressed with the work that Gertrude and Mary Ann were doing last night? He howled almost the whole time they were in the parlour."

"I didn't really hear him except as background noise," said Lydia. "I wonder if the ghostly energy can extend as far as the barn?"

"You'll have to ask Gertrude," said Jane. "In the meantime maybe we could take him over to Ian's when they're working here." She slid a tray full of cookies into the oven. "They're coming again this evening to see if they can get a better grasp of whoever Julia is."

The little band of ghost hunters arrived about nine o'clock just as the sun was setting. "This is a good time to get here, and I had a nap this afternoon when I put the baby down." Gertrude unbuckled the car seat from the hooks holding it in place and lifted it out of the back seat, then picked up the diaper bag. Don released Roddy from his safety harness and helped him out of the car. In a few minutes Mary Ann and big Jim drove in and skidded to a halt in a spray of gravel. Mary Ann was driving her car. It was her preferred method of transportation.

She didn't like it when other people drove and Jim did not seem to mind her haphazard driving skills. He peeled his large frame out of the front seat of the red mini and stretched.

"Fast ride, Jim?" teased Don.

Jim chuckled. "You betcha. Sit down, hang on and say your prayers."

"Oh, c'mon Jim, it's not that bad. I've never had an accident yet," said Mary Ann. Her hair stuck up in points all over her head where the wind from the open window had blown it. She licked her fingers and slicked them through the mess.

Gertrude headed toward the house. Don took Roddy by the hand and turned toward the back door. Roddy hung back tugging on Don's hand and pointing to an upstairs window. "Don't want to go in there tonight, Daddy." His voice was wobbly and tears were not far behind.

"Why not?" asked Don.

"Someone's up there." He continued to point toward the side of the house.

"Where?"

"Up high. In the window."

Don searched the various windows with his eyes, but could see nothing. "Which window?"

"Up there. The one with the black trim."

Don looked again. "There's no window with black trim, Roddy."

"There is! There is!" Roddy's voice rose to a screech. He pulled his hand out of his father's grasp and ran back to the car. In seconds he was in the car with the windows rolled up and the doors locked.

"C'mon Roddy, there's no one there. Open the door."

Roddy tried to make himself small in the corner farthest from his father. He shook his head and began to cry hard.

Don turned toward the house and went to find Gertrude. "Roddy's locked himself in the car and won't come out. He says there's someone in an upstairs window."

"We weren't upstairs," said Gertrude.

"Which window was it?" asked Jane.

"I don't know. He said it was the one with the black trim. I didn't see any that had black trim."

Jane physically startled. "That's the attic window and it hasn't been trimmed in black for years. All the windows used to be trimmed in black until Grandma decided that she wanted red trim for a change, then the last time they painted, they just did everything white. Grandpa and she had a disagreement over the trim colour, and he got mad and painted everything the same colour."

"We have to get into that attic," said Mary Ann.

"I called the locksmith today, and he said he couldn't come until next week unless it was an emergency," said Jim.

"I'd say this is an emergency," said Gertrude. "I've got a kid locked in the car and a ghost on the loose and dear knows who else is here of a ghostly disposition. Where are Charlie and Ian?"

"I took Charlie over to Ian's this afternoon and I don't know where Ian is right now," said Lydia.

The telephone rang and everyone stood staring at it as if they'd never seen one before. It rang again. Jane hurried to pick up. "Oh, hi, Ian. Where are you?"

"Charlie's having a major temper tantrum and I don't know what to do with him."

"Oh, dear. You maybe should talk to Lydia. We have our hands full here just now. I'll put her on."

Jane handed the phone to Lydia. "It's Charlie."

Lydia listened and un-hunhed a few times then said: "I guess you'd better bring him home and we'll lock him in the barn again. It seems to be his 'safe' place." She set the phone in its cradle, then turned to the group. "Charlie's in an awful state and he's got Cedric all stirred up too. Ian's bringing him over and locking him in the barn for me. I guess I'd better put some food and water out for him." She picked up Charlie's water dish to fill it with fresh and poured a new bowl of kibble. "That dog!" she muttered under her breath.

In a few minutes Ian's black pickup truck rolled into the yard with Charlie in the passenger seat. Ian came to a stop and snapped a leash on Charlie's collar. Charlie braced his feet and whined.

"C'mon, Charlie, stop the nonsense." Ian tugged on Charlie's leash. Charlie wouldn't budge. Ian picked him up bodily and carried him into the barn, unhooked the leash and shut him in. Charlie howled.

In the house Jim said: "I guess Charlie doesn't like it here much better."

"Now we know how far the ghostly influences reach," said Lydia just as Ian stomped into the porch. He entered the kitchen.

"That dog! He just would not stop."

"Tell us about it. We've now got an unhappy canine locked in the barn and an unhappy boy who's locked himself in the car and won't come out," said Don.

Gertrude and Mary Ann exchanged glances. "It's a good night for ghosties," said Mary Ann. "Let's get started."

"So what are you going to do first?" asked Jane.

"Mary Ann and I had a brief telephone meeting this afternoon," said Gertrude. "We decided that our best approach is to try to contact Julia again.

We want to know, if we can find out, who she is. Then depending on what she tells us, we can decide where to go from there. It's too bad the locksmith can't come until next week, I think the answer may lie in the attic."

"I searched through all the boxes of Grandma's stuff again today but I couldn't find anything," said Jane. "The 'junk' drawer was no help either. Actually, the two of us looked in every place we could think of, but we didn't find anything useful."

"Did she have a bank box?" asked Jim. "She may have kept it in there."

"She did, but I and the lawyer emptied that just after the will was read. We closed the account."

"So that's a dead end too," said Mary Ann. "Darn! I was so hoping."

"Let's you and I go into the parlour now," said Gertrude. "If we're lucky we'll make good contact and be there for awhile. Keep your eye on the baby, Don. There are diapers in the bag and a bottle of milk."

The two psychics took themselves off to the parlour and turned on some side lights, then settled themselves in the two armchairs and prepared to trance. The shadows seemed thicker this evening and the air was somehow denser. They closed their eyes and focused their minds. In the ladies' chair in the window a whiteness appeared just as the last rays of the setting sun quieted into darkness.

"Julia?" asked Gertrude in her mind. The whiteness took on the shape of a woman. She sat very upright in the chair and settled her skirts around her ankles. She then looked directly at Gertrude.

"What do you want of me?" The sound seemed to echo in Gertrude's mind and spill into the physical. Mary Ann jumped, then relaxed.

"Why are you here?"

"I've come for my coat."

"What coat?"

"Freddie won't give it to me."

"Who's Freddie?"

"Not me."

"Your name is Julia?"

"I told you so, didn't I?"

"You did," agreed Gertrude. "Can you tell me your last name?"

"I don't need a last name. Everyone knows who Julia is." She began to fade.

"Don't go, Julia," said Gertrude. "Stay and visit awhile."

The figure seemed to brighten. "Where's Jane?" She disappeared and Gertrude and Mary Ann were left staring at an empty chair.

"Darn!" said Mary Ann. "And she was much stronger this evening."

"I know," said Gertrude. "I was hoping that she'd

tell us something useful. We need to get into that attic soon."

"So do we call it quits for this evening?"

"I guess we have to." Gertrude rose from her seat and stretched. "I'll see if Jane remembers anything more. Maybe she knows who Freddie is."

They returned to the kitchen. Out in the barn Charlie still wailed with unhappiness.

Jane turned from her task. "Anything new?"

"Nothing. Not even a last name. She said she didn't need one, that everyone knew who Julia was," said Gertrude. "By the way, d'you know who Freddie is?"

Jane smiled. "That must be Grandma she was talking about. Her nickname was Freddie, short for Frederica."

"Sounds like an opera star," said Jim. "I wonder if there's anything in the newspapers from that time that could give us a clue. I'm going to the archives tomorrow for another case I'm working on. I can start a search then."

"Maybe Gertrude can help you and the two of you can dig up more information together than alone," said Don. "We have one more business day before the weekend. I can mind the baby if you want to go out for a couple of hours. I have a light day at the office tomorrow and I know that my reception-ist would love to have her to herself for awhile."

Gertrude ran her fingers through her hair. "If she really wouldn't mind. It will be much easier if I don't have to look after her while I'm trying to research. She's very good but ... " Her voice trailed away as she looked over at Lydia cuddling a sleeping baby in the rocking chair.

"It's all arranged, then," said Don. "I'll take the baby tomorrow morning, you can do your work and I'll bring her home at lunch time."

"I'd better check on Roddy," said Gertrude. "I don't know why he's so spooked this time. He never has been before." She pulled a flashlight from the kitchen drawer and switched it on. "I'll see if he'll come in now. I thought he'd be more help given his 'gift,' but maybe you should just stay home with the kids for awhile until he settles down." She turned to go. "I'll ask him if he wants to come in now."

She picked her way across the dooryard by the dim light of the flashlight. The car door stood open and Roddy was nowhere to be seen. A shiver of alarm ran through Gertrude as she ran her light around the yard. "Roddy! Where are you?" She hurried back into the house. "I can't find him," she said, then hurried back out, her flashlight bobbing over the gravel as she ran.

Don and Jim followed. "You don't suppose he'd try to walk home?"

"I'm not sure he'd know the way." Gertrude was

panting after her run across the yard. "Roddy! Roddy!" she called. As she neared the barn she could hear Charlie whining softly almost as if he were talking to someone. Gertrude pulled open the door and shone her light inside. The only part of Charlie that was visible was the end of his nose, the rest of him down to the tip of his tail was covered in straw. He barked once and began nosing around where his belly should be. Presently he uncovered Roddy. He was tucked in between Charlie's fore paws sound asleep and Charlie looked as if he were cuddling him in his big doggie embrace. He looked up at Gertrude and whined.

"Oh, Charlie, you're a good dog to look after Roddy so nicely." Gertrude ruffled Charlie's ears. "Thank you." She went to the door and called Don. "I've found him. C'mere. You've got to see this. Be quiet or you'll wake him."

"For goodness sake. Who'd have thought? Charlie has been so freaked by the energy I wouldn't think he had it in him."

"I guess we'd better wake him," said Gertrude. "I wonder how long he's been out here?"

"I figured he'd fall asleep in the car," said Don, "so I just left him." Don bent to pick up Roddy. Charlie whined. "I feel a little guilty leaving him in the car like that but there's not much he can get into out here and it was getting dark."

"No harm done," said Gertrude. "He's smart and pretty independent. When he's properly wakened up we'll ask him."

Don gave Charlie's head a scratch. "Good dog, Charlie."

"Wuff," said Charlie.

Together they made their way across the yard. All the downstairs lights were on. Gertrude held the door for Don. "I wonder where they all went, and where's the baby? She's gone basket and all." Alarm sounded in Gertrude's voice. She hurried to the hall and shouted for Jane.

"Where's the baby?" she asked when Jane had appeared.

"Lydia's got her. There was a crash upstairs. We didn't want to leave her alone while we investigated. Did you find Roddy?"

Gertrude took a long, deep breath and nodded. "He was in the barn with Charlie."

Lydia rounded the corner of the dining room with the baby in her basket. She was still sleeping.

"Did you find out the source of the crash?"

"No. We looked everywhere. It must have been in the attic," said Jane.

The back door banged on its hinges. Jim and Ian came in. "You found him. Good. We looked everywhere outside," said Ian.

"We even went over to Ian's to see if he'd gone

over there," said Jim.

"Thanks guys," said Don. "Really appreciate it. I thought he'd really gone missing."

"He did,"said Gertrude. We certainly didn't know where he was. And we've got to find a name for the baby. If she ever got lost, we wouldn't know what to call her by."

Chapter Five

The next morning Gertrude entered the old brick building on Richmond Street. It took almost an hour of searching through old copies of The Guardian to locate even a mention of anyone named Julia. They were being micro-fiched and were slightly disarrayed. She almost missed the ad for a performance of *La Bohème*. It was one night only because the star, Julia, had another engagement with the opera in Moncton. It seemed to be a very quick tour of the Maritimes before winter set in. Gertrude searched the ad with a magnifying glass but could find no reference to Julia's last name. She searched the newspaper for the day following the performance and found a front page story, above the fold, about the event including the names of the supporting cast. Her stomach tightened when she saw just a first name, "Erica," as the maid and confidante of *La Bohème*. She was described as a local talent. "Aha," she muttered to herself. "So if that was Grandma, she probably did know Julia! I must ask Jane if her Grandmother's used a slightly different first name for privacy purposes on programs and posters."

"Shh!" scolded the patron at the next table. She was a wrinkled old woman with what appeared to Gertrude to be wearing a woollen cap. She was reading and taking notes.

"Sorry," whispered Gertrude. She read farther in the article. So Julia played Musetta, thought Gertrude. What did Grandma play? She read farther. Grandma understudied Julia for the performance, besides being her maid, she thought. Wow! Grandma must have been quite a singer in her day if she was chosen to understudy the star. I wonder who understudied the maid? Gertrude finished reading the article and discovered that Julia was able to take a few days rest on the Island before the engagement in Moncton and she was staying with a friend from the cast. I wonder if the friend from the cast was Grandma? Gertrude's thoughts ran on to the possibilities as she closed down her search.

That evening the little band of ghost hunters gathered at Jane's for strawberry shortcake and real whipped cream. "Ian brought over some fresh cream right after milking," said Jane. She ladled generous spoonfuls over the sweet biscuits and berries. "It gave me the idea for the shortcake, so we have Ian to thank for our delicious treat this evening."

A chorus of thank you's rose around the table as they each took their first bites. "This is so good," said Mary Ann, "I just love fresh strawberries and cream." She patted her rounded tummy.

"I'll have to run an extra mile to wear those calories off," said Jim.

"G'way with you," said Mary Ann, "you don't run."

"We'd better get on with our project or we'll be here 'til midnight," said Gertrude. "I left Don home to mind the baby. I'll start." She told them of her discoveries of the morning. "What was your Grandmother's first name? I found an entry for a local woman but she was only called by her first name and I wasn't sure."

"Grandma's first name was Frederica," said Jane. "She went by Freddie a lot. She didn't seem to like her first name much. I asked her once why she didn't like it. She kind of brushed it off with some remark about her misspent youth. I didn't know what she meant and the way she shut her lips so tightly I knew better than to ask any more questions."

"In the article there was a woman who was called by Erica, but it didn't give her last name. It just said she was local."

"So Grandma may have had at least that much of a career in opera," said Jane. "I never knew." She turned to fill the kettle for tea then set it on the stove still hot from supper.

"Maybe they didn't want you to know," said Mary Ann. "After all, in those days stage acting was still considered a little too far out there for nice girls." She ran her fingers through her wind dishevelled hair.

"I'd forgotten that," said Gertrude. "She'd have been on the outskirts of society. How did people regard your grandma?"

"I don't really know." said Jane. "I never even got a whiff of anything like that when I was a child. Of course, they were awfully good at keeping those kinds of things from children. I don't think they'd have been as successful with the neighbours so there might have been talk. You'd have to take into account my grandfather's role in all of this too. He wouldn't have stood for any social nonsense from anyone."

"He was also the one with the still during Prohibition," said Jim. "So anything that was being said would have been kept pretty quiet or he'd have heard it and done something about it."

"Maybe that's what happened the time that Little Billie had something to say in front of Grandpa," said Jane. The kettle came to a boil and Jane added water to the tea bags and set them on the back of the stove to steep.

"Who's Little Billie?" asked Gertrude. She rose from her chair and began to distribute napkins around the table.

"He was a neighbour boy who used to play with me when we were children. I don't remember what he said, it was just a hint and sounded kind of sly. Grandpa went after him and gave him such a talking to I felt sorry for him. Anyway, Billie was sent home that evening and he was never allowed to come back."

"Where is he now?"

"In town somewhere, I think. He's not Little Billie anymore. He gained an awful lot of weight but he still goes by Little Billie though, or so I've heard. That day I was forbidden to ever play with him again."

"He's in town running a a shop catering to ladies and gentlemen of a certain kind," said Ian. "I saw him a few weeks ago and he's bigger than ever. He is looking rather dissipated, but I guess it kind of goes with the territory. He had a wife but she left. He never said why. I could visit him and hear what he had to gossip about. We'd at least know what the neighbours had to say back then."

Gertrude pulled mugs out of the cupboard and began pouring tea. "By the way Jane, Julia asked after you last night. She said quite distinctly, 'Where's Jane?' I forgot to tell you."

Jane set the jug of milk on the table with a little crash. Her face went as white as the milk that splashed over the edge. She gave a sharp intake of breath before asking: "Did she say what she wanted me for?"

"No. She faded from sight just then. Did you know her?"

Jane had been holding her breath and let it out in a rush. "No. If I've ever met her, it was before I can remember."

"Hm," said Gertrude. "If you've never met her I wonder why she thinks you should have been there?"

"Maybe she's never very far," said Mary Ann. "From what I've been reading, there's some evidence that the so-called other side is right here, superimposed on our reality. It's all just a matter of levels of spiritual vibrations. We, in our dense bodies, don't vibrate at their higher level but sometimes they can lower themselves to ours with the right person."

The air suddenly thickened. "That's right," said Molly quite distinctly. "You were looking for me, Gertrude?"

Gertrude's eyes took on a far away look and she looked somewhat sleepy. "Molly, you're home! Where have you been? I've called a number of times but you've never answered."

"Humph!" said Molly. "I need a vacation now and again. All work and no play makes Molly dull. Larry and I went to the Bahamas for a few weeks.

Larry organized a conference for new spirits and I helped him, and let me tell you it was a lot of work. Those new ones, especially the teenagers, whew! So what did you want me for?"

"We have a situation on our hands here. A spirit who won't tell us anything but just keeps whining about looking for her coat. We've researched and tranced to not much avail. We can't seem to contact Grandma although she does appear from time to time but never says anything, just stands there, glowers at us and then fades. We think there might be information in the attic but it's locked and we can't find the key."

"So you've got a haunted house and you don't know how to handle it," jibed Molly. "Gertrude, Gertrude, of course you can handle it. But I'm here now and you don't need me. You're on the right track. The answer is in the attic. Julia did know Grandma. The coat she's looking for is in the house practically under your noses. What you need to look for is Grandpa's doings in all this and it will all become clear. Goodnight."

Gertrude shuddered and sat up straighter in her chair. She opened her eyes to find everyone staring at her with wide eyes. It seemed to Gertrude as if no time had passed. She picked up the conversation where she had left off.

"Like me and Mary Ann," said Gertrude. "It's

weird that only certain people can see these things, never mind communicate with them. I think everyone has a certain ability but if you ignore it and don't develop it, it goes dormant. A few years ago I'd have made a u-turn rather than acknowledge I had any gift in that direction. My mother had a little and faked the rest but I have a much stronger power than she had. He has an even stronger gift than I do." She nodded toward the lounge where Roddy was fast asleep.

"Does Don have any?" asked Lydia. She had been silent for quite some time. Now she asked: "Are you more spiritual than the rest of us? Don't get me wrong, I don't mean for that to be a rude question."

"No, but he's very supportive," said Gertrude. "And protective. As for being more spiritual, I don't really know. For myself I don't think so. I go to church. I may have a broader understanding of spiritual matters but who's to say what's spiritual and what is based on science and we just don't understand yet."

"How did you develop yours?"

"I came in kicking and screaming, so to speak," said Gertrude. "I thought I was going crazy. I didn't want to be like my mother who was, in fact, a little off the rails. Molly had a great deal to do with it from the other side. We work together now. Then Don came along and tested me for every kind of

insanity he could think of and could find none. So
the only conclusion we could come to was that the
experiences I was having were real."

"Who was Molly in real life?" asked Jane.

"She was a patient of mine." Gertrude picked
up her fork. "She and I used to strike sparks off
one another when she was on this side. She'd had
a stroke and had problems speaking so I had the
upper hand in any conversation we had. She didn't
like that. So when her friend, Lucy, came back and
taught her how to astral travel, she got back at me
by playing ghostly tricks on me. I worked the night
shift so she had a full eight hours to harass me. It
was when she started to follow me home and create
mental havoc there that I went to see Don. I almost
ran out the door when I saw him. I went to school
with him and his secretary. I didn't want him dig-
ging around in my psyche, and the secretary was
the school's worst gossip. However, it all worked
out, and look at us now, two children later."

"So how did you meet Jim and Mary Ann?"
asked Lydia.

"Through Don," said Gertrude." Jim and he were
high school friends. Jim went the psychic route
and Don went the psychological route. After all the
probing of my psyche Don decided that Jim was a
person I should know. So off we went, and Mary
Ann lived across the field from Jim, and she was a

psychic and Jim's friend, so I met her too. She was the one who educated me in other-worldly realms and taught me to trance." Gertrude smiled across the table at her friend and tutor.

"Who also wants to know what Molly had to say when you 'left' us for five minutes?" replied Mary Ann. "Where has she been?"

Gertrude sighed. "I tranced, did I? It's no wonder that you were all staring at me. I wondered."

"You were gone for over five minutes and you were muttering and sighing and making faces."

"Molly showed up. She was a little peeved at me for being so persistent. And I was peeved with her for not letting me know she'd be gone and for how long. Her peeve outdid my peeve so all I really got from her was that we are on the right track and that Grandpa is the key to it all."

"How in the world can we ever research Grandpa?" asked Ian. "All of the old people are dead and their descendants are scattered and probably don't know anything except gossip anyway. They were all so tight lipped."

"There are ways," said Jim. "I'll get on it.

Over the next few days Gertrude continued her search for Julia but could find no further reference to her anywhere. She finally gave up on the Island newspapers and called The Toronto Star. They managed to find an entry in the social pages commenting on *La Bohème*. The cast was an illustrious collection of theatre elite from across Canada, and the star, Julia, was from Paris. She was described as lovely in face and figure with the voice of an angel. The opera house was filled with the members of upscale Toronto, with some coming from as far away as North York and some of the other outlying communities. Their evening attire was described in great detail as well as hairdos and accessories. The orchestra was the best that Canada had to offer.

"There's a picture here too," said the archivist. "I might be able to copy it and mail it to you. Will that be helpful?"

"That will be perfect," said Gertrude. "I've been searching for that sort of thing for weeks now. I haven't even been able to discover her last name."

"I believe it's Montblanc but from the looks of things she never used it. According to this, she said she didn't need to, that everyone knew who Julia was."

"You have done me a great service," said Gertrude, "and I thank you sincerely." She gave her address and telephone number. "I look forward to receiving this."

"I found out Julia's last name," said Gertrude at suppertime the next day. "It's Montblanc and she's from Paris. I am so excited!" She scooped a chicken breast from the dutch oven and put it on Don's plate, added some vegetables, mashed potatoes, and a ladle full of tomatoy-looking gravy.

"How'd you manage that?" Don spread his napkin across his lap, then glanced at his plate. "What's this? A new dish?

"Coq au Vin. I saw it in a magazine at the library yesterday and I thought I'd try it. The vegetables were my idea." She prepared a plate for herself and took her seat at the table. "I finally called the newspaper archives in Toronto and the archivist was able to locate the information. She's sending a copy of the article and the picture that goes with it."

"Well done," said Don. He picked up his fork and prepared to spear a carrot. "Will that make your sessions with her from the other side any easier?"

"Maybe, maybe not." Gertrude slid into her place at the table and spread her napkin. "I don't know if she'll be cross that I uncovered her last name or not. Now maybe I can find out a little more about her. I wonder if the library at UPEI will have anything on early 20th century opera." She spooned a small serving spoon of mashed potatoes onto Roddy's plate and set it in front of him. "I'll go tomorrow and see what I can find out."

Gertrude's visit to the library the following day produced a small entry in the encyclopedia of music. "So she had a bigger ego than renown," muttered Gertrude to herself. She didn't make much of a splash in the bigger picture, she thought. I wonder why not. Can I find that out? Maybe if I visit the music department. She returned the book to the librarian at the circulation desk. She was a buttoned up woman in a twinset and grey straight skirt. Her glasses hung by a black cord from around her neck. "Excuse me, I wonder if you can help me?" said Gertrude. "I want to consult with one of the professors about an opera matter. Who should I ask to see?"

The librarian pulled up her glasses and perched them on the bridge of her nose. She peered at Gertrude as if deciding whether she should part with a name. "Professor Macdonald is likely your best bet. He's been here for donkey's years and knows an awful lot. He's over in the music building."

I hope this man's approachable, thought Gertrude. She trudged across campus carrying the baby in her car seat. She thought back to her days in Nursing School. Her few excursions onto campus were not happy ones. I hope he's here today. She pulled open the heavy door to the music building. The professors' names and room numbers were displayed in a closed case on the wall. She found Professor Macdonald's room number easily. Butterflies tickled in her stomach. It was a leftover reaction from her days as a student when she was summoned to the Head Nursing Education office.

She came to the correct room number and could hear a voice from within and see the top of a partially bald, grey haired head through the top clear glass pane in the door. She rapped on the wooden door frame.

Professor Macdonald rose, opened the door and waved her inside while continuing with his telephone conversation. He gestured toward the one chair at the end of his desk. Gertrude seated herself and settled the baby in her carrier by her feet. Presently the professor ended his call and greeted her. "And who might you be?" His voice was harsh with years of pipe smoking although there was no evidence of it in his room. He was a tweedy looking man who chewed on a mangled toothpick.

"I'm Gertrude." She stuck out a freckled hand. "I want to ask if you know anything about early

Canadian opera."

He shook hands briefly. "That depends," he said. "What do you want to know?"

"Have you ever heard of an opera singer named Julia who sang here for one performance at the turn of the century?"

He chewed hard on his toothpick for a moment, further crushing it. "I suppose you mean Julia Montblanc."

Gertrude's eyes lit up. "Yes, that's who she is."

"Was," said Professor Macdonald. "She's long gone. She was here for one gala evening once in her life. Why do you want to know?"

Gertrude looked down at her hands currently folded in her lap. They had tightened to white at the knuckles at his question. She forced them to relax. "I'm researching her."

"Yes, but why?"

"A friend of mine said she stayed with her grandmother all those years ago and my friend got curious."

Professor Macdonald pulled the soggy toothpick from his mouth and tossed it into the trash. "I suppose your friend is too busy to do her own research." He reached for the dispenser of toothpicks and retrieved a fresh one. He inspected it for splinters before popping it into his mouth. "Please excuse this nasty habit. I've been ordered to quit smoking and this is my first week without. I've been replacing one unpleasant habit with another." He turned his attention back to Gertrude. "So. Your friend. Is she lazy?"

"No." said Gertrude. "She just acquired her grandfather's farm and she's trying to figure out the stories she's heard about her grandmother over the years, only no one was ever allowed to talk about it. She thinks the house might be haunted."

"Typical. You'll need a psychic to figure this one out." He leaned back in his chair. "However, you have not answered my question. Why you and not her?"

Gertrude swallowed hard. "Because I am the psychic."

"So why ask me? Don't psychics have access to everything?"

"No. That's why I'm researching it. I was at the archives this morning and I'm unable to find out anything besides her last name and the fact of her having been here. I've been talking to other archivists across Canada and no one has been able to tell me anything. So I thought maybe ... " Her voice trailed away.

Professor Macdonald turned in his chair and reached for a small book with a dark blue cover on his bookshelf. He leafed through it and then handed it to her open. "This is the only reference

I have on her. There are her birth dates and her death dates and the fact that she was a singer of some talent who emigrated from Paris at the turn of the century."

Gertrude skimmed the information. "I know this already. I'm interested in her career. She certainly seemed to have had one. She thought that she had great renown, but I'm beginning to think it's mostly ego. She was certainly eager to tell me that everyone knew who Julia was."

Professor Macdonald sat up straighter in his chair and chewed harder on his toothpick. "You've been talking to her?" Excitement filled his voice.

"She comes and goes," said Gertrude. "She comes through and says a few things and then fades. She's very elusive." The baby stirred briefly in her carrier then settled again. Gertrude leaned over and tucked her blanket more securely around her feet.

"That's quite a talent," said the professor. He watched Gertrude closely to discern her sincerity. "Think what you could do if you could talk to Bach or Beethoven."

"I doubt I could access them," said Gertrude. She straightened in her chair. "I have no reason to, and they would have to want to talk to me too. Otherwise the energy won't work." She thought a moment. "I've never actually tried to contact anyone famous, and who would believe me anyway?" She rose from her chair. "I thank you for your time. If you think of anything else let me know." She handed him her card with only her first name and a post office box number on it.

Professor Macdonald looked at the card. "No telephone?"

Gertrude smiled slightly. "There are a lot of crazies out there and I don't want to be bothered by them." She picked up the baby carrier. "My mother thought she had 'the gift' and it was very hard to live with growing up. The other children would taunt me and I don't want that to happen to mine."

Professor Macdonald finally smiled. "And you really do have 'the gift'."

Gertrude nodded a little crookedly. "So does my son. Even more so than I do."

"So you have to be careful."

"It's lovely to have an evening to ourselves," said Gertrude. She nestled into the crook of Don's arm and patted his knee. Despite the summer weather Don had built a small fire in the fireplace. Roddy played with his cars on the floor. Twilight shadows played over the bookcase and danced through the leaves on the tree outside, their reflection skipped over the hardwood floors and made spatters of dark and light on the cream coloured wall. On the floor Roddy played 'Cops and Robbers,' pushing his cars this way and that. The baby was already asleep upstairs and the baby monitor was on alert next to Don.

"We have to think of a name for her soon," said Gertrude. "It's kind of ridiculous to just call her the baby as if she doesn't belong to us. People are starting to ask and we have to get her baptized soon."

"R-r-r, I'm the police and you bad guys had better stop." Roddy pushed his pretend cop car with some speed across the floor. It bumped off a baseboard and rolled to a stop. "Not like that!" he scolded the imaginary policemen. "You're supposed to catch them, not let them get away." He crawled over to the car and sent it off after the bad guys again. "They have a head start on us, sir. We'll never catch them now."

"I've been thinking about that too," said Don. "Charlotte keeps springing to mind. I always thought that it was such a pretty name. I had a little girlfriend in kindergarten with that name."

"Charlotte it is then. What about a second name? She'll need one of those."

"How about Hope?"

"Charlotte Hope." Gertrude sounded the names together. "That's a nice combination."

Just then there was a serious accident between Roddy's police car and the truck it was chasing.

"Oh, oh, sir, I think that was bad crash. We'd better call the ambulance," said Roddy.

"I think he's been watching too much television," said Gertrude.

"Where's he watching that stuff?" asked Don.

"I don't think he is. He doesn't spend much time at other kids' houses so he wouldn't have access to that. It's mostly cartoons and kiddie shows when he does watch it here."

"His pretending is pretty Keystone Kops."

Gertrude chuckled. "I'll ask him when I put him to bed. It's almost time." She sighed and stretched. "I hate to get up just now. This is so cozy."

"I'll be here when you get back," said Don.

"C'mon, Roddy, it's time to put the bad guys to bed. The policemen have to have some sleep too." Gertrude knelt down beside him on the floor and helped him corral the various cars and Lego buildings he had created for his imaginary world.

The living room was put back to rights and Gertrude herded Roddy up the stairs. She monitored tooth brushing and clothes folding and bedtime prayers. "Is there anyone at school you want to be grateful for?" asked Gertrude.

"Maybe Kenny." Roddy yawned. "He's poor and the other kids don't like him. He doesn't know how to play."

"How do you mean?" Gertrude looked intently

at Roddy's face.

"He smells funny, and he talks like 'thith.'" Roddy imitated a lisp. "He has a scar on his lip too. The kids think he's funny looking. But I don't."

"That's good," said Gertrude. "Was he the one who taught you how to play cops and robbers?"

"Yeah, it's fun." Roddy yawned again.

"What does the teacher think of that game?"

"She doesn't like it. She told us not to play it and once she took the cars away from us. But that didn't matter, we played with stones instead."

"I see," said Gertrude. "Was that the right thing to do?"

"I don't think so. I felt kind of wiggly in my tummy, and I was afraid that teacher would catch us. She's nice but she could punish us."

"Is there another game you could play with Kenny?"

"I don't know very many. The girls know a lot more than the boys do."

"D'you know how to play 'Blind Man's Bluff,' or how about 'Simon Says'?"

Roddy shook his head. "The girls play 'Simon Says' but they won't let the boys play."

"I see," said Gertrude. "The boys should start their own games."

"They still wouldn't let Kenny play and I wouldn't want to leave him out."

"Does Kenny live nearby? Maybe you could invite him to come over to play after school some day."

"Could I, Mommy? That'd be super." Roddy yawned again. "I want to go to sleep now."

Gertrude tucked the blanket more closely under Roddy's chin and gave him a goodnight kiss. "Okay. See you in the morning."

She pulled the bedroom door half shut and turned out the light, then went to check on the baby.

She went quietly downstairs. "I think the baby is good for another hour or so." She settled herself on the sofa in her former position. "I asked Roddy where he learned about the Cops and Robbers game. He said he learned it from Kenny."

"Did he say what Kenny's last name is?"

"No, and I didn't ask."

"I wonder if it's that family that lives in that rental unit over on Broad Street? They have a kid called Kenny. The children are out on the street at all hours. I don't think they're very well cared for."

"Roddy did say he smelled funny and that he lisped and had a scar on his lip."

"That's probably why he lisps. If he had a cleft lip when he was born, he might have had a cleft palate too. Maybe they weren't properly repaired."

"M-m," said Gertrude. "That would certainly explain the lisp. I told Roddy to bring him home after school someday."

Jane and Lydia were just drying the last of the lunch dishes when Jimmy Gaudet came roaring up the lane in his ancient van that lacked a muffler. Gravel scattered as he came to a stop at the back door. Charlie added to the din by barking and straining on the end of his tether under the tree. He had been warming his joints in the afternoon sun and enjoying his doggy day. A noisy truck was outside his current level of knowledge. Jimmy scrambled down from his seat and slammed the door. He pulled off his battered, oil-stained hat as he bent over to scratch Charlie's ears and make friends. "I'm sorry for the noise, dog, but I hit a pothole in town the other day and it took off my muffler and I haven't had a chance to get it fixed." Charlie sniffed Jimmy's outstretched hand and discovered a chewy treat. It sealed the friendship. "Is your Mom inside, dog?"

"Wuff," said Charlie and licked his chops.

"They're vitamins," said Jimmy. "Only one a day. Sorry, dog." He turned and made his way across the yard. He knocked on the door and stepped into the shadowy porch. "Anybody home?" he called. He rapped on the kitchen door. "I'm Jimmy, and I'm here."

Jane opened the door. She drew breath to greet Jimmy but it was taken away by the scene of him standing there, hat in hand. He smoothed a long untrimmed beard, grey in patches around the edge, with the other hand. He stuck out a less than clean hand calloused by years of hard work. Jane automatically stuck hers out in return.

"C'mon in, Jimmy. I'm Jane and this is Lydia. I heard you meet Charlie."

"I did. I always carry a few doggy vitamins in case I meet up with a cross one."

Jane chuckled. "Good idea, and Charlie's not cross, he just thinks he's a guard dog."

"I could tell. His tail was going like a windmill in a hurricane. You have a lock you want picked?"

"Yes, in the door to the attic. I've lost the key and I need to get in there. Squirrels, don't you know." Jane turned and led the way upstairs.

"They can chew an attic out in no time. You'll need to see where they're getting in and block their passage."

"I'll get it cleaned up there and find their routes," said Jane. She climbed to the little landing on the outside of the door. "Here it is, and I don't think it has been opened for years."

"H-m," said Jimmy. "It looks like the original lock. This is going to be a puzzle." He rummaged in his tool box and extracted a slender instrument and stuck it in the lock. "There's something blocking the hole." He poked around a little and frowned in concentration. "I think I'm going to have to take this apart and remove it altogether." He poked around a little more. "Yup, yup, yup, that's what I'll have to do." He pulled the slender instrument out of the hole and put it back in his tool box. "It's okay with you if I take this apart? There aren't any screws on this side to take out so I'll have to break in."

Jane nodded. "It doesn't need to be locked anymore, there are no children around."

Jimmy grabbed a screw driver from his box of tools and extracted the lock after some effort. He inspected it for its construction. "This is a vintage lock, about 1923. They were very sturdy and quite expensive in their day. Aha! There's what was blocking it. It looks like someone stuck a wad of putty in the hole and it hardened. I wonder how long it was like that and who would do such a thing?"

"Dunno," said Jane, "I just know that they didn't want children in there. I've never been up here. I was never allowed."

"How'd they keep you out? If it had been me, I'd have gotten in by hook or by crook when I was a kid."

Jane chuckled. "They told me that there were ghosts up here and they were mean and would eat us. Of course, we believed them."

"There's the reason you couldn't find the key. It was pushed under the door by whoever was up here last."

Jane rolled her eyes and shook her head. "Who knows? Probably Grandpa or Grandma."

"I guess they really wanted to keep people out."

Jimmy gathered up the bits of lock. "I have a new lock set in the van I can replace this with." He went out to the van to get it and was back momentarily. "I don't suppose you want this old one, do you? I collect antique locks and I'd like to have it. There's probably a story about its manufacture somewhere."

"It's no good to me. You can have it."

"Thanks," said Jimmy. He set about installing the new lock. He was finished in no time and presented the key to Jane with a flourish. "I'll invoice you at the end of the week." He collected up his tools and was soon rattling and roaring down the gravel lane.

Jane went back to the kitchen. "Now that I have the attic open, I don't know if I want to look up there alone."

Lydia looked up from the book she was reading. "Why not? That's all we've been talking about for weeks." She put her bookmark in place and set the book beside herself on the lounge.

"I'm not sure." Jane made a face. "It sort of feels

like an invasion of privacy now that I can. Grandma was so protective of it all her life. Besides, I don't want to go up there alone." She looked hopefully at Lydia. "I don't suppose you're up for a little exploration?"

Lydia looked at Jane. "You're not afraid, are you?"

"There have been a lot of strange noises coming out of there these last few weeks. It almost feels like there's something up there that wants my attention."

"Why don't you call Ian? I think he'd be glad to come over. Especially if you offered him some fresh rhubarb pie." Lydia looked at Jane out the corner of her eye and smirked.

"Oh, stop it! I'll have to wait until he gets in from the field before I call him anyway."

"That'll give you just enough time to make the pie and cool it."

Jane sighed. "I guess it's you who wants some rhubarb pie." She set about collecting the ingredients, then went out and pulled rhubarb. In a few minutes she was back indoors with an armful of rhubarb stalks. She dumped them into the sink. "You could be useful and wash these while I chop them." She set the plug and filled the sink with water.

Lydia set her book aside and began washing the long, red stalks. "We used to make hats out of the rhubarb leaves when we were little. D'you remember that?"

Jane smiled at the recollection. "I do. We had such fun that summer."

"We even made little hats for our dolls. What was your doll's name? I remember I called mine Georgina."

"Mine was Suzy Bee with a zed. No Susie's for me. D'you still have yours?"

Lydia shook the excess water off the stalks of rhubarb and handed a bunch to Jane. "I do have her. She's sitting on the top of my dresser in that little pink shirt I made for her out of scraps from Mom's sewing basket. D'you remember your grandmother warning us severely not to eat the rhubarb leaves?"

Jane began chopping rhubarb. "Yes. She was quite adamant about it. I remember daring you to take a bite of the stalk. You almost threw it up it was so sour. Grandma never did say why we weren't to eat the leaves."

"I looked it up once. It said there were oxalates in them that would poison the kidneys. They tried using them in England during the war for greens and people got sick from them before the doctors could figure out what was causing the illness."

"I wonder if Grandma knew that?" Jane chopped another bundle of rhubarb and scraped it into a bowl. "Probably not specifically. She knew an awful lot of things but none of it with any scientific foundation. She just knew it, so she didn't do it and wouldn't let us do it either."

Lydia made a face. "If the leaves are as sour as the stems, who would want to eat them, raw or cooked?"

Jane scraped the last of the chopped rhubarb into the bowl and dumped in two cups of sugar, then added an egg and two tablespoons of tapioca. She stirred it up with a couple of shakes of cinnamon out of the cinnamon jar. After a few minutes of mixing and rolling she had the pie crust made and shaped in the bottom of the pie pan. She dumped the rhubarb mixture in after, vented and added the top crust. She fluted the edges and declared it ready for the oven. Soon the aroma of cinnamon permeated the kitchen. "I wonder if I should call Gertrude and tell her we got the attic open? I don't think she was expecting that until later in the week."

"Give her a call," said Lydia. "She's either busy or she's not. And don't forget to call Ian too," she teased.

That evening the ghost hunters gathered in Jane's kitchen. Jim wasn't able to make it. Ian was the last to arrive and came bearing a bottle of rum. "Joe gave me this a few weeks ago. I don't generally drink but I thought since this was a momentous occasion we might need a sip to steady our nerves. Otherwise, you can use it for fruitcake."

"Or mincemeat," said Jane.

"Or mincemeat," agreed Ian.

"Maybe afterwards," said Gertrude. "I like to keep my wits about me when I may want to go into trance. It's not a state I want to be in without them. You can mind Charlotte, Don? I'll take Roddy with us. He likes attics and dusty places. Besides, he sees things that we might miss."

"I'll stay here and keep Don company," said Lydia. "I don't like dusty places."

"What about you, Jane?"

"I'm coming with you. I'm not going to pass up a chance to find out what Grandma was trying to hide."

"I'll come too," said Ian. "I can catch Jane when she faints."

"I've never fainted in my life," said Jane. She sniffed and stuck her nose in the air.

Together they all climbed the stairs to the attic.

"I suppose we'd better knock before we go in," said Mary Ann.

"It's only polite," said Gertrude.

Mary Ann rapped on the door. "Anybody here?" she called.

Gertrude startled as the sound of rushing wind

sifted through the cracks.

"I'm scared, Mommy," said Roddy. "I don't want to go in there."

"You don't have to. You can go back down with Daddy," said Gertrude. "But why don't you want to? We've talked about this before, and you know that spirits can't hurt you."

"Kenny's brother said so, and Kenny's afraid of ghosts now."

"Were you telling them about being able to see them?"

"I didn't want to, but Kenny's brother made me. He said you were a witch."

"Well, you know I'm not."

"I know," said Roddy. He hung his head and looked sad. "And even if you are, you're a good one."

Gertrude's lips tightened. "I don't want you having anything to do with Kenny's brother any more. You can play with Kenny, but don't let his brother bother you. When do you see him, anyway?"

"Only at school. He comes on purpose to find me and Kenny. He's in grade seven. In the fall he'll be in grade eight. I don't like him. I tried to run away once and he grabbed me by the arm and wouldn't let me go. I'm glad school is out now."

"Where was the teacher? Why didn't she intervene?"

"She was looking the other way. I guess the

eyes in the back of her head were shut, so she couldn't see."

Gertrude shook her head. "Kenny's brother shouldn't be on the second graders' playground at all. You go back to Daddy if that's what you want."

Roddy ran back downstairs.

"I'll have to have a word with the teacher." She turned the door knob carefully and pushed the door open slowly. "Is there a light switch handy?"

"Try inside the door," said Jane. "It's probably about shoulder height. The switches in this house are quite high."

Gertrude fumbled around the edge of the door jamb and felt for the switch. The light poured forth from the two bulbs, one at one end of the attic and one at the other. The evening shadows were more or less dispelled, and with the remaining rays from the setting sun filtering in through the dusty end windows, there was just about enough light to see by. Gertrude pushed the door open wide. "Wow!"

Mary Ann peered over her shoulder. "I agree with you. Wow!"

The attic was finished with wood panelling and the floor was made of scrap lumber and shellacked to an almost shiny finish. A braided rug covered the centre of the floor. At one end of the attic there were racks of sequined dresses and feather boas in every hue. A shelf held old-fashioned hats in every colour of the rainbow with ribbons and plumes to decorate. An armchair in the other corner with a small table and a reading lamp beside it completed the tableau. A book of plays lay open face down on the arm of the chair. A cup that had once held tea sat on the table, green with ancient mould. It seemed to have been forgotten in a hurried departure. Across the room there were two trunks and a dresser.

Jane gasped at the opulence and secrets the attic held. "I almost hate to enter. This was Grandma's secret place and she didn't want anyone else in here."

"We're here now," said Gertrude. "We've come this far to find out so we had better start looking for whatever it is that Julia wants. I think the answer is here." She stepped over the threshold. A gust of wind blew through the attic. She felt the tug of an entity trying to make contact. The pull was very strong. "I need to trance," she said. "Come with me, Mary Ann."

"I'm right here," said Mary Ann. She sat down cross-legged on the floor and shut her eyes. Gertrude was already far into her psychic realm. "Don't go so fast," Mary Ann called to Gertrude. Gertrude stopped and began talking to someone unseen. Mary Ann arrived in the same level of trance that Gertrude occupied and saw her talking to a middle-aged woman with silver hair.

"I don't know who you are," said the vision. "Who let you in here? Where's Jane? She knows better than to let anyone in here. This is my secret place." The vision seemed to throb with indignation growing larger and smaller, then larger again almost as if it were breathing.

"Jane let us in," muttered Gertrude. "We want to know what Julia wants."

"And you think you'll find it up here, do you?"

"Yes," said Gertrude. "D'you know what she wants?"

"What she always wanted. Fame, fortune and adulation."

"Can I give it to her?"

"She'll drain you dry."

"This is a beautiful room," muttered Gertrude.

"I made it for me," said the vision. "No one is allowed up here but me."

"Not even your husband?"

"Not even him. He agreed."

"What was his name?"

"Angus," said the vision. "He was a good man."

"So what's your name?" muttered Gertrude.

"Freddie."

"So are you Angus' wife?"

"Who else would I be if Angus is my husband?"

The vision began to fade. Gertrude sighed deeply

and opened her eyes. "I think it was your grand-mother," she said to Jane. "She doesn't like us being here. She said she never even let her husband come in here."

"That sounds like Grandma. Did she tell you what Julia wants?" asked Jane.

"Not exactly." Gertrude rose from her seat on the floor. "She just said 'fame, fortune and adulation' and that she'd drain me dry trying to get it."

"That Julia must have been quite the diva when she was alive." Mary Ann stretched.

"I got the impression from what I was able to find out from my researches that her ego was bigger than her talent," said Gertrude. "The light is fading. We should see what we want to see and get back down stairs. You can do some more exploring tomorrow, Jane."

Jane picked up the dirty cup and carried it downstairs.

Chapter Six

The next morning it was pouring rain. Charlie was howling in the barn.

"This is a good rain," said Jane. "Grandma always said a rain like this was good for the garden."

"It's not good for dogs though," said Lydia. "Just listen to Charlie."

"You'd better go get him and bring him in. He'll howl himself hoarse if he keeps that up. There's a raincoat behind the door in the porch."

A few minutes later Lydia was wrestling Charlie into the porch. "C'mon Charlie, you're not staying out in the rain. You know you don't like being wet."

Charlie sat down at the open threshold and refused to budge.

"Charlie, it's either here or the barn." Lydia held his leash taut so he couldn't back up.

"He's having a fine fit," said Jane. She shook the bag of treats she had brought with her. "C'mon Charlie, it's treat time, but just in the porch." She shook a doggie treat just out of Charlie's reach, then another one a little farther away, then another after that.

"Wuff," said Charlie and gobbled up the treat closest to him. "Wuff." He sat down on his haunches. "Wuff."

"Here's another," said Jane. Her voice dripped with enticement.

"Wuff," said Charlie and did not move.

"Oh, c'mon Charlie," said Lydia. She tugged on his leash. "Stop the nonsense." She turned to Jane. "I'll grab his collar and you push from the rear. He's too heavy to lift."

Jane did her best to force Charlie into the porch. Lydia slammed the door behind them with her free hand.

"That is one stubborn dog," said Jane. She brushed wet dog hair off her apron. "He can stay here until he dries off."

She went back into the kitchen. Behind her she could hear Lydia scolding Charlie. "You're going to go to the kennel if you keep behaving like that here. No more car rides for you. No more playing with Cedric. Now go lay down."

"Wuff," said Charlie. He hung his head and slouched over to his blanket.

Lydia joined Jane in the kitchen. "Honestly, I don't know what's gotten into him this morning."

"Maybe there are some vibes left over from last night. Or maybe he knows what we're going to do this morning." She hung the dish towel behind the stove to dry.

Lydia made a face. "He's too smart for his own britches sometimes."

"He's in now. Maybe he'll stay settled for awhile."

"What're we going to do today?" Lydia settled herself in the rocker and picked up her magazine.

"I know what I'm going to do," said Jane. "I'm going up to the attic and see what I can find." She put the last teacup into the cabinet. Upstairs a door slammed. They both startled and Charlie howled. "I can see that someone isn't too pleased with that idea."

"Maybe we shouldn't," said Lydia. She set her magazine back in the rack beside the rocking chair. "Maybe Grandma won't like it."

"She's a ghost. What can she do to us?"

"We don't know what she's capable of," said Lydia. "Nor that Julia one either. Maybe we should wait for Gertrude."

Jane pursed her lips. "No. Grandma has been dead for months now and Julia has been dead for much longer. This is here and this is now and this is my house. I shall do what I want in it."

"We could call Ian and see if he's free," said Lydia. She smiled slyly at Jane.

"Will you cut that out!" said Jane. "Next thing you'll be saying something in front of him and embarrassing us both to death."

"Just a suggestion."

Jane was silent for a few minutes making work around the kitchen. "Maybe I should call him and see if he can come over. I don't fancy Grandma and Julia if they get really angry." She picked up the phone and called Ian's number. He answered on the first ring.

"Is something wrong, Jane?"

"Not yet. We're going to explore the attic, and Charlie's in the porch howling, and the door upstairs just slammed and scared the wits out of all three of us. Can you come over?"

"I'll be there in ten minutes. Don't go near the attic until I get there."

Jane hung up the receiver. "He'll be here in ten minutes."

"See, that wasn't so hard, was it?"

Jane ignored Lydia and pulled the roast from the refrigerator. "I'd better get this started before we go upstairs or we won't be having any dinner today."

Ian arrived in a spray of gravel and red puddle water. "C'mon, Cedric. Time to go in and see Charlie."

Cedric whined.

Ian prepared to make a dash for the house. "C'mon, Cedric, a little rain won't hurt you. You've got your all-weather coat on and Charlie needs your company today. You'll have the back porch to your-selves." Ian grabbed Cedric's collar and pulled him across the bench seat of the truck, then picked him up bodily and carried him into the house. He set Cedric on his feet on the floor and gave him a gentle push in Charlie's direction. Charlie was huddled on his dog blanket where he had hauled it into the corner. His paws were over his eyes.

"Arf," said Cedric, then cuddled down next to Charlie on the blanket.

Ian took off his boots and hung his raincoat on the hook behind the door and went into the kitchen in his stockinged feet.

"Good morning, Ian." Jane finished drying her hands and hung the towel on the rack over the bottom cabinet door to air dry.

"Any more noise from upstairs?" asked Ian. His dark hair was wet and plastered to his forehead. He pulled the kitchen towel from the rack behind the stove and wiped the rain from his brow.

"No," both women said in unison.

"This house has had a restless feeling ever since the door slammed," said Jane.

"And Charlie has been howling and whining in the porch ever since I brought him in," said Lydia. "Since before that, really. That's why I brought him in."

"But it hasn't helped," said Jane.

"I brought Cedric over so he should keep Charlie

company and maybe he'll be quiet."

Jane made a face. "Maybe they'll both be howling." She gave the counter one last wipe then turned. "Are you guys ready to go upstairs?"

"I guess so. I don't really want to, though," said Lydia.

"You can stay here," said Jane. "I won't be alone upstairs."

"No, but I will be down here. Besides, I don't want to miss all the fun."

Together the three made their way upstairs. Footsteps sounded overhead. "Now, who's up there?" muttered Jane.

"More to the point," said Lydia, "how'd they get in there? The front door is locked and they would have had to go past us to get in."

"I'm almost afraid to go up and see," said Jane.

"I'll go first," said Ian. He climbed the short flight to the attic and opened the door. The footsteps stopped. He flipped the light switch and climbed the interior stairs and looked around. "Wow! Who'd have guessed your grandma had such exotic taste?" He looked around. "There's nothing here," he called. "C'mon up."

Jane and Lydia climbed the last few steps. Rain drummed on the roof but the underlying silence was profound. "It sure is quiet up here. Almost too quiet."

"Well, let's get exploring," said Lydia. "The faster we find something, the faster we can get downstairs again."

Jane looked around herself then pulled the closest box toward her. "I'm going to start with this box. It seems to have old essay books in it."

"Maybe it's from your grandmother's school days," said Ian.

Jane opened one and glanced through it. "I don't think so. They seem to be old journals. Come to think of it, I sort of remember her writing in them when I was little." She began counting the notebooks. "There are ten here. That doesn't seem like very many for a whole lifetime."

"Perhaps there are more elsewhere," said Ian. "I'll carry this box downstairs and you can look for more."

"I'm going to look in the trunk," said Lydia. "I think trunks are fascinating."

"Those journals had fairly recent dates on them and they were closest to the stairs. There must be more nearby," said Jane. She scrambled to her feet and looked around. "What's that over there?" She opened another box that had been set on top of a stack of boxes in the corner. "More journals by the look of these."

Ian picked up the boxes one by one and carried them downstairs.

Lydia pulled the trunk away from the slant of the eaves so she could open it. Something seemed to fall behind it. "I think I may have knocked something behind here." She closed the trunk lid and peered behind. "It looks like a poster." She handed it to Jane.

Jane unrolled the poster and found several others inside. "Would you look at that! Posters for the upcoming opera." She scanned the announcement. "There's Grandma's name. She was the star in this one."

"What about the others?" asked Lydia.

"Here's the one where she understudied Julia." Jane unrolled the smallest of the collection. "This must be where she started first."

"Those things are historically priceless," said Ian. He looked over Jane's shoulder. "We didn't have opera here often, I don't believe. There weren't enough people who could sing like that."

"I wonder how Grandma got her training?"

"They did have singing lessons at one time," said Jane. "Everyone would gather in the schoolhouse in the evening and be taught by singing teachers from town. I remember my grandfather talking about it. He was rather scornful of the whole business because he couldn't carry a tune in a hand basket. I don't think he liked the teachers who led them either because they were all men, and Grandpa had very rigid views on how women should behave and who they should associate with, no matter how chaperoned they were."

"Women were so hemmed in those days. Singing lessons in large groups were one of the very few things they were allowed to attend outside of church. Of course, it was a good place to meet the boys too. If it had been me I'd have been kicking over the traces every chance I got," said Lydia.

"No, you wouldn't have," said Jane. "You'd have gotten a bad name for yourself in no time. Grandma used to be here in the summertime. This is where she became acquainted with Grandpa. Grandma kept sneaking out to see Grandpa until her father sent her back to Toronto to stay with his sister for a year. I think he was hoping the whole relationship would blow over. Great Aunt Jane, the one I was named for, was quite strict, so the story goes. There were also stories about her in her youth which could explain why, and why she was living in Toronto.

"C'mon, open the trunk. You've got me curious." Jane helped Lydia open the heavy trunk lid. "Goodness! Will you look at that?" Jane began to rummage through what appeared to be stacks of folded material.

"That's not just folded material," said Lydia, "it's evening dresses."

"Is that a jewellery box in the corner?" asked Ian. He pointed at a wooden box half hidden under the dresses.

"It's probably the accessories that go with these dresses," said Jane. "Grandma was very stylish even in her aprons. She could do amazing things with scraps of this and that. I always admired them when I was little." She picked up a dress and shook out the folds. "Wow! It's no wonder Grandpa kept a tight lid on gossip around here. Bad enough that he had a still during Prohibition, but to have wife who worked in the theatre. I wish my mother was still alive, I'll bet she could tell stories."

"Maybe she wouldn't, either," said Ian. "She was probably taught that you don't tell the neighbours anything." He frowned. "Remember how your grandpa treated Little Billy? She wouldn't have dared. By the way, I tracked down Little Billy. He doesn't remember much about the incident, just that he wasn't allowed to come over any more."

"Like everyone else around here, none of them remember anything." said Lydia. "I remember once when I was little, I told someone about one of our family affairs and got caught and thoroughly scolded for it. I never opened my mouth again."

"So that's why you were so guarded when I met you."

Lydia nodded. "It has hampered me all my life.

I still feel guilty saying anything. I even feel guilty about snooping around in this attic."

"Truth to tell," said Jane, "so do I. Grandpa must have had an awful hold on the community to have such control over everyone's loyalty like he seems to." She began rummaging again and found a particularly handsome dress in peacock blue. She held it up to her. "Isn't this a stunning dress? I just love the colour."

"It looks good on you," said Ian. "Matches your eyes." He turned quickly away so that they couldn't see the embarrassment in his. His tanned face reddened slightly around the edges of his chestnut hairline.

Behind his back Lydia shot a look at Jane as much as to say, "I told you so." She jumped to her feet and looked at her watch. "Look at the time. I'm parched. I'm going to go down and put the kettle on." She hastened away. Downstairs Charlie and Cedric howled in unison. Lydia scrambled back up the narrow attic stairs. "I don't think I want to go down there alone."

Jane sighed. "We'll each take a box and we'll all go down together. Charlie and Cedric can go out in the barn."

"I wonder what's bothering Charlie out here. I never took him for a 'fraidy cat," said Lydia, "and he's done nothing but whine and complain since he got here." She picked up a box of books just as the trunk lid slammed shut. Everyone startled and Lydia dropped her box. "Let's just get out of here." She grabbed up the box of books again and headed downstairs.

The rain had stopped for the moment and Charlie and Cedric still howled in the porch. Outside the yard was dotted with red mud puddles and daisies. The sun tried briefly to penetrate the cloud cover but soon disappeared.

"I'll put the kettle on and you guys can drag Charlie and Cedric out to the barn again," said Lydia. "I left my rain boots in town."

Jane set her box down on the window seat in the kitchen. "Did you think it never rains out here? It's not Camelot, you know." She stepped into the porch and pulled on her boots and yellow raincoat. "You can be in charge of making tea, then." She shut the door behind herself and Ian.

Together they leashed the dogs and found they had to drag them every step of the way. "What is wrong with you two today?" said Jane. "You are so stubborn when you want to be, Charlie."

"Cedric's not much better," said Ian. He hoisted Cedric up onto his shoulder where Cedric buried his snout and eyes in Ian's neck. "He's trembling!"

"He must be really frightened." Jane pulled and pushed Charlie into the cattle barn. He looked up at her with pleading eyes. "Never mind the pity party, Charlie. You don't like it in the house and you don't like it out here." Jane tied Charlie's leash to a stanchion. "You can stay there until I can put down some more hay for you and Cedric to snuggle under."

Ian tied Cedric beside Charlie. "I'll get them some fresh water. They can stay there until we've gotten them settled and the door shut." He picked up the bucket and headed for the pump. Soon the screech of the pump handle could be heard above the howls of the two dogs.

Jane climbed into the loft and forked down some hay. That should be enough with what's already down there, she thought. She glanced up to the peak window and in the light of the grey day and in the dust she'd stirred up moving the hay she saw the figure. "Grandpa! What're you doing here?" She continued to stare at the misty figure. It wavered and held out a misty hand to her. "What do you want? Why are you scaring the dogs?"

The figure smiled and faded. Down in the stall where they had tried to retreat, Charlie and Cedric howled. Jane slid down the ladder and landed right at Ian's feet. He held out his arms to steady her. His warm bulk was reassuring and Jane briefly snuggled a little closer then jumped back in embarrassment. "I-I shouldn't have done that," she said and scuttled out and began piling hay around the dogs, her cheeks a little rosy from the encounter.

"What shouldn't you have done?" asked Ian. He followed her into the stalls. "You shouldn't have come that close to me? You didn't have much choice, I was right there." His lips quirked into a smile that he tried hard to suppress. "So what shouldn't you have done?" He put his hand on Jane's shoulder and turned her to face him.

"I shouldn't have taken advantage of your comfort like that." Jane hung her head but peeked up at him out of the corner of her eye. "It's just that I guess I've been under more stress than I realized these past few weeks."

Ian smiled broadly. "You can take advantage of my comfort any time." He opened his arms wide and Jane snuggled into him for real this time. He put his arms gently around her slender body and held her to him. He kissed the top of her head. "Who were you talking to up in the loft?"

"Grandpa was there." Jane snuggled a little closer. "I'm going crazy, aren't I?"

"I don't think so," said Ian. He tipped her chin back to look into her blue eyes. "There have been some very strange things happening here lately, so I don't think you're going crazy. Because if you are, so am I."

"And the dogs, too, I suppose," said Jane. She

looked steadily back at Ian.

"The dogs too." He bent his head and kissed her gently on the cheek then released her.

"We'd better get the dogs settled and get back. Lydia'll be wondering where we've gotten to."

"If she asks, what'll we tell her?" asked Ian.

"The truth, if she asks," said Jane. "Settling the dogs and talking to Grandpa."

Jane and Ian sloshed across the muddy yard just as the heavens opened again. "We're going to need to build an ark if this keeps up," said Jane. "I've never seen such rain." She jumped over a puddle that she knew from experience was particularly deep.

"Shall I bring my hammer and nails the next time I come?" asked Ian, who had chosen to wade.

Jane laughed. "Maybe you should."

They entered the porch. Jane shook the water off her raincoat and toed her wet boots off into the tray. "These can drip dry for awhile. I don't plan to go anywhere else today."

Together they went into the kitchen.

"I got the vegetables ready for the pot," said Lydia. "The tea's on the stove. Does anyone want a cookie?" She looked back and forth between the two of them. "What took you so long? I was beginning to worry."

"It took us awhile to get the dogs to settle. I went up to the loft and forked down some fresh hay for them while Ian got them water. They're not a bit happy."

"Is that all?" Lydia quirked an eyebrow at Jane.

"I think I saw Grandpa up there too," said Jane. That bit of information deflected Lydia from her line of questioning.

"What did he look like?" Lydia threw her wet dishcloth back into the soapy water and turned to face Jane. "C'mon, tell me more."

"He was pretty dusty, but I had just stirred up the hay when I threw it down for Charlie and Cedric so it may have just been a trick of the light. I saw him against the light coming in the gable window."

"Did you talk to him?"

"I just asked him what he was doing here and why was he scaring the dogs."

"Did he answer you?"

"No. I wish he had. He just smiled and faded away."

"It wasn't just your imagination?"

"No. He's my grandpa, after all. He was one of my favourite people all my life."

"So it really was your grandfather." Lydia stared hard at Jane trying to figure out what was real and what she might be making up. She turned to the stove and lifted a pot lid and stuck a fork in the contents. "These are done, I think." She tried the carrots. "These'll be done by the time I set the table and mash the potatoes."

"I'll set the table," said Jane. "Has the gravy been made?" She began setting three places.

"Just before you came in." Lydia carried the potato pot to the sink and drained it, then began mashing them with unusual vigour. "I wonder if we should be messing with spooks and spirits at all," she said at last. "The dogs are scared out their wits, you're seeing ghosts, there are strange noises here night and day, and neither we nor Gertrude can get to the bottom of it. Maybe we should quit."

"The so-called spooks and spirits are messing with Jane," said Ian. Upstairs a loud crack sounded. "Now what?" Ian stalked toward the hall in his stocking feet and headed upstairs. He found nothing amiss. He returned to the kitchen.

"Julia just wants her coat back, according to Molly" said Jane. "Apparently it's here somewhere." A bell tinkled from the parlour as if in approval. They all startled.

Lydia shut the hall door to try and block the sound. "We're not listening just now," she called softly into the daytime shadows of the parlour. "Why haven't we found it?" she asked the others.

"I don't know, I just have a feeling that this house holds a secret." Jane looked at Ian. "I have no idea what it is, nor where to look for it. And now we've got bells ringing in the middle of the day."

"I've been thinking that same thing lately," said Ian. "When is Gertrude's next visit?"

"Tomorrow evening."

"That'll give us time to start reading Grandma's journals," said Ian.

"D'you want to do that kind of grunt work?" asked Jane.

"Heck, yeah. I'm kind of invested in this now too. Besides we'll get through them faster with an extra pair of eyes."

"Sit in then," said Lydia. "The sooner we eat, the sooner we can get started."

After dinner Ian pulled the rocking chair over and sat and propped his feet on the open oven door, then began reading while Jane and Lydia tidied the kitchen. Jane walked around him several times when she was clearing the table. "You look just like Grandpa there, Ian. He used to sit with his feet on the oven door a lot, especially in the evening."

"Uh-huh," said Ian, "I remember." He glanced at Jane and then went back to his reading.

Jane and Lydia washed the dishes and put them away, then each took a box of notebooks and were soon engrossed in history. There were notes on weather and crops and visitors. The notes on the visitors were the most interesting because Grandma was an astute observer of her fellow humans and recorded it all. Occasionally Jane read one of her grandmother's descriptions and chuckled. Some of the people she remembered well and a few she had only met, and most of them were very old now or very dead. Never was Grandma far wrong in her assessments although she seldom shared with anyone except her notebooks.

"I wonder if the neighbours knew what she thought of them?" said Lydia. She had just read a particularly acidic account of a man who lived on the next farm. He was lazy and didn't keep his fences in good repair. His cows had gotten loose into Grandma's pristine garden and made a salad bar of the greenery.

"Old Sam probably got his ears blistered that time," said Jane. "Grandma took great pride in her garden and after that incident Grandpa put up a fence around it. He didn't apologize for Grandma either, if I recall. It was one summer when I was staying with them. I helped Grandpa with the fence. He made a picket fence and I 'helped' him paint it."

"I think I remember you painting the fence with him," said Ian. "If it's the time I remember, I came over after chores to play and Grandpa sent you off with me. You had more paint on you than you had on your patch of the fence."

"That's right," said Jane. "I remember now. You took me down to the creek and dared me to jump in. You called me a 'fraidy cat for not wanting to do that. You taunted and teased until I did jump in just to shut you up. I remember I hit the bottom and over-balanced and fell all the way in. I was soaked and the water was so cold."

"You didn't speak to me for the rest of the summer either," said Ian. "You were so mad and you had to go back to your grandmother and tell her what had happened."

"Yes, and she laughed and then scolded me for being so gullible."

"Did she use the word gullible?" asked Lydia.

"She did, and I didn't know what it meant, and that made everything worse. It was years before I could even spell the word so I could look it up." She turned a page to continue her reading.

Lydia pulled the cushion from behind her back on the window seat and punched it into a more comfortable shape, then pushed it behind herself again. "I love window seats but they do have their drawbacks," she muttered and began reading again.

The three continued reading in silence. The afternoon darkened into evening around them and the birds in the trees across the yard chirped sleepily and then quieted. In the barn even Cedric and Charlie were quiet. Jane reached across and flipped the light switch and went back to reading. "Here's something interesting," she said. "I'm reading one of the books from Prohibition. She says: 'The government boys were here today. I'm glad Angus was out back, he's not a very good liar. They wanted to know if the reports they had heard about there being a still out here were true. And did I mind if they looked around? I told them to go ahead but don't touch the boiler in the cellar. It heated our water and I was planning a big wash this morning. Those boys only glanced at it and since it was clean and smelling like soap they didn't go any farther with it. Fortunately for Angus he'd just finished a run and everything was scrubbed clean and shiny and, of course, the boiler was the still, but I was heating water in it for the wash.' I guess Grandma wasn't an actress for nothing."

"So Grandpa never got caught?" asked Lydia.

"I don't think so," said Jane. "He always seemed to know just when those guys would show up and be conveniently out back in the woods when they came. Of course, Grandma would always cover for him. She had these big blue innocent-looking eyes that could be as hard as rock when she needed them to be. She was kind of a chameleon that way."

"Your grandma was a real character," said Ian. "I used to be half scared of her when I was really little. If you weren't here to play with, I wouldn't come over at all. Then they'd all tease me about being sweet on you."

Lydia stretched and swung her legs over the edge of the window seat. "I've had enough reading for tonight."

"At least the dogs were quiet," said Jane. She got out of her chair and put her book back in the box. "Anyone for a cuppa?"

It had been a busy night but the house was very quiet the next day, although the atmosphere felt as if it were still waiting. "Sweet relief," muttered Lydia. She dumped dry dog food into Charlie's bowl then squelched her way across the still puddled yard to the barn. "Charlie, breakfast," she called. The pile of hay never moved. The barn felt empty. "Charlie, where are you?" She began pulling handfuls of hay off the pile. "C'mon, Charlie, up and at 'em. It's breakfast time." She cleared the stall almost to the back and only found one chewed rope where Charlie had been. "Darn that dog. Where did he go?" she grumbled to herself.

In the house the phone rang. Jane answered. It was Ian.

"Are you missing a dog?" he asked.

"I don't know," said Jane, "did you find one?"

"Charlie's here. It looks like he chewed through

his rope and came to visit Cedric. I found them together in the woodshed this morning."

"Lydia's just gone out to feed him. It's quiet now, but there was a lot of activity here last night. It was hard to sleep. Maybe he'd just had enough and decided that a sleep-over with Cedric was necessary. I'll tell Lydia."

"So it was noisy there last night, was it?" Ian seemed reluctant to end the call. "All night?"

"For about an hour around three o'clock. I thought the ghosties would never go to bed. I figured it would be useless to get up and look for them so I stayed in bed. Lydia joined me about half way through."

"Cedric just had to go out about then. The rain had stopped and I knew he could find shelter in the shed so I just let him go. He headed straight for the woodshed."

"That must have been about the time that Charlie ran away. Here's Lydia now." Jane turned toward a breathless, dishevelled Lydia. "Are you missing a dog?"

Lydia pulled bits of hay from her hair and threw them in the trash. "Yes, and when I find him I just might strangle him! Has someone found him?"

"He's at Ian's with Cedric. Apparently they had a sleep-over."

Lydia plopped down into the rocking chair. "At

least he didn't go far. Wretched beast!" She sighed. "I'll go get him after breakfast. I'm starving."

"Did you hear that, Ian?"

"There's no need to come here, I have to go to town this morning, I can drop him off on the way by."

"Thanks then, Ian. We'll see you in a bit."

A short while later Ian's truck crunched to a stop in Jane's yard. Charlie and Cedric sat on the bench seat as if they belonged there. Their tongues lolled as they panted away the warmth of the summer day. Ian climbed out of the driver's seat and grabbed Charlie's collar. "C'mon guys, let's go for a visit." Charlie would not budge and Cedric growled. Ian picked up Charlie bodily and set him on the ground then led him out to his safe haven under the spruce trees. Ian went and slammed the truck door leaving the window open so Cedric could please himself. "I'm going into the house to see if the girls need anything."

"Good morning, ladies. I brought Charlie back. Any chance for a cup of coffee?" He shut the kitchen door behind himself.

"I can make some quick enough," said Jane. She rose from the rocking chair where she had been reading The Guardian, filled the kettle and plugged it in. "We had a cold breakfast this morning, it was so hot already. I hope instant is okay."

"Whatever's going." said Ian. He settled his bulk at the kitchen table. "So you had a noisy night last night. Nothing broken and no one hurt, I hope."

Jane spooned coffee crystals into mugs. "No, nothing like that. Just noisy. At one point I thought I heard Grandma's voice telling someone to stop, that it might frighten Jane."

"So, she's sort of looking out for you?"

"It seems so, if what I heard was really there to be heard." Jane plopped down in the rocking chair again and sighed. "I swear, I think it's getting noisier here by the night. If Lydia hadn't joined me, I would have joined her."

Lydia made a face at Jane and slid off the window seat. "Charlie needs some water and some food," she said "I'll be back in a bit."

"You both look tired. You especially," said Ian. It surprised him how much he longed to take Jane in his arms and somehow make things better for her. He cleared his throat and turned his head away.

Jane poured boiling water into two of the cups and did not see. "If we don't get to the bottom of this soon I'm going to have to go back to town and only come out here in the daytime."

Ian cleared his throat again. "I'd miss you."

Jane turned startled blue eyes on him. "Would

you?" She picked up the coffee cups and set them on the table. "I think I'd miss you too." She turned quickly toward the refrigerator to get the cream.

"When's Gertrude coming back?" Ian reached for the little pitcher that held the cream.

"This evening. She called earlier and said that Don could look after the baby and that she and Roddy would be here."

"Can I come too?" His expression took on a boyish look of almost pleading.

"Of course, you can. I wouldn't think of doing this without you anymore." She dumped two spoonfuls of sugar into her mug forgetting that she'd already sugared it liberally.

Lydia came into the porch, loudly banging the door behind herself. She kicked off her boots and came into the kitchen. "Charlie and I had a very long talk about the niceties of going visiting without an invitation, especially in the middle of the night."

"D'you think he listened?" Ian laughed.

"More to the point, do you think he knew what you were talking about?" asked Jane.

"He was pretty hangdog when I was done," said Lydia. She helped herself to the hot water. "Whether he understood or not is another matter. He wasn't the brightest pup in the litter."

"Did you notice what Cedric was up to?" asked Ian.

"He was taking a nap on the seat. He raised his head briefly when I looked in, then went back to sleep." Lydia sat down at the table and helped herself to cream and sugar.

Ian rose. "I have quite a few errands in town so I should be on my way. Is there anything you need there, Jane?"

"No, I have to go in to my apartment anyway and water the plants. I haven't been there since the end of last week so they'll be getting pretty dry by now. I've been so busy here I haven't even picked up the mail."

"I could do that for you," said Ian. "You would have to give me the address and the key." His tone was eager. "Then you wouldn't have to make the trip at all."

"Thanks, Ian, but I need to get away from here myself. It's almost as if I can feel pressure building up here and I don't know what it is. I'm going to ask Gertrude this evening about this."

"I'll see you this evening, then." Ian turned away. "Thanks for the coffee."

Lydia watched Jane out of the corner of her eye. "That man likes you. A lot."

Jane ignored her and busied herself washing out coffee cups with her back turned to Lydia. She studied the cup that Ian had used and wondered.

Gertrude and Roddy arrived just before sunset that evening. Ian arrived shortly thereafter.

"I left Cedric home this evening," said Ian. "He doesn't like being here when the spirits are abroad. If you like, Lydia, I can take Charlie across and put him in the shed with Cedric."

"Would you? That will be a great help," said Lydia. "He's such a nuisance here and I have to be always half aware of where he is. I tied him in the barn earlier. If he keeps chewing his rope I won't be able to tie him at all."

"Perhaps he needs a chain," said Jane. "I could have picked up one in town this afternoon if I'd thought."

"He needs obedience school," said Lydia. "He's getting more and more unmanageable."

"As I understand it, he's had quite a disrupted summer," said Gertrude. "Maybe he just needs to settle into a familiar routine again. He's quite a sensitive dog, you know."

"Can I go out and talk to him, Mummy?" asked Roddy. "Maybe he'll tell me what's bothering him." Roddy turned appealing blue eyes on Gertrude.

"You know where Ian's is and you know where we'll be. You know he's in the woodshed. Don't get into anything."

"I know, Mummy, I won't. You'll come and get me when it's dark?"

"Of course! I won't leave you there to get home by yourself. Now go. The sun has already set. I'll watch you across the fields."

Roddy took off at a run and was soon at the top of the hill at Ian's back field. He turned and waved and then disappeared over the crest of the hill.

"He's getting so grown up," said Lydia.

"Too grown up sometimes," said Gertrude. "He's a reliable kid all the same."

"Ian's house and barn are pretty kid-proof anyway," said Jane. "He has nieces and nephews who come out from town from time to time."

"I didn't know that Ian had brothers and sisters," said Lydia.

"He doesn't. These kids are the children of his cousin but they call him uncle."

It was almost dark when Ian returned. "I got Roddy and the dogs settled. I showed him where the spare key was to the house so he could get in to the phone if he had to. I also gave him one of those electric lanterns so he wouldn't be completely in the dark if we don't finish here when we think we will. The dogs were all over him when I left."

A thump resounded from upstairs.

"I guess it's time," said Gertrude. "Our guests have arrived." She turned toward the stairs and took a step into the hall. She was stopped by an invisible barrier at the parlour door. Jane and Lydia fetched up behind her. Gertrude regained her balance and glanced into the parlour. A light was forming in the ladies' chair by the window. It grew and expanded to fill the whole chair taking on the form of a woman in long skirts as it did so. Gertrude held her breath.

"I think she wants me in the parlour," whispered Gertrude. "I can already feel her mentally. Ian, keep watch at the door. You two go back to the kitchen. She seems to like Ian's presence this evening."

Gertrude stepped into the parlour and sat down in the chair opposite the light. She was already partially in trance and was having a hard time keeping her eyes open. Soon she gave in and opened to the apparition. "Julia?"

"That's me," said the ghost. "I have a little more energy this evening. You are a strong generator. Your friend not so much."

"D'you mean Mary Ann?"

"She's a little flighty and hard to siphon from."

"What can I do for you this evening?"

"You're reading your grandmother's diaries. Look in the one from 1905." She wavered a little as

Gertrude sighed and stirred. "Sit still for a minute. You already know that I want my coat. It's a silver fox fur. It was a gift to me from a wealthy lover. It was stolen in Halifax at the Neptune. I left my door unlocked and someone took it. It's in the secret closet now." Julia began to fade and soon was gone from sight.

Gertrude stirred. "I wish you'd told me which closet," she muttered. "I've been through every closet in this house." She stretched and rubbed her eyes then rose from her seat.

"Did you find out any more?" asked Ian. "I could hear you muttering and sighing but I couldn't hear what you were saying. Are you okay?"

"I'm fine," said Gertrude. "Just a little thirsty. Let's convene in the kitchen."

In a few minutes they were all assembled around the kitchen table.

"So what did you find out?" asked Jane.

"I was talking to Julia again. She was much clearer tonight. For some reason she doesn't care much for Mary Ann. She said she was too flighty and interfered with the flow of energy. She said I was a good generator. Have either of you read the journal from 1905 yet? She said the coat was in a secret closet somewhere in this house."

"I was reading at random," said Lydia. "I don't think I got back that far yet."

"Same with me, sort of," said Jane, "although I did start from the first one. Some of the entries were pretty sketchy when she first started. She did start journaling a lot when she first started to sing professionally. She still hadn't met Julia when I had to stop and make supper and I never got back to that particular era."

"I haven't read very many of them at all," said Ian. "I certainly didn't read anything about Julia or a fur coat."

"Have you gone through all the closets yet, Jane? Julia said it was in a closet. I can't imagine where they could conceal a closet big enough to hold a fur coat."

"Yes, but I haven't found a fur coat. I'll go through them again just to be sure. I doubt I would have missed something as precious as a period fur coat."

"It must be here somewhere or she wouldn't have been so insistent."

"We'll have to look for it in the daylight." said Gertrude. She rose. "I have to go and get Roddy. In the meantime, someone read the 1905 journal, please."

Gertrude found Roddy perched on the top step of Ian's back porch. His elbows were on his knees and his chin was in his hands. He looked quite forlorn.

She sat down beside him.

"Have you been waiting long?"

"Not long."

"Are the dogs in the shed?"

"Yes. They're in the corner and they wouldn't come out. I asked them why and they just said they were afraid of ghosts. They weren't any fun so I came out here. There are a lot of little bugs around. They bite so I went in with the cows for awhile. They were all laying down chewing something and only one wanted to talk. I asked her if she ever talked to the ghosts and she said they didn't even know them."

"Did Charlie or Cedric say anything else about the ghosts?

"No, They just said that one of them was looking for her coat and we weren't looking in the right place even though one of them pointed it out to us. There's one that lives in Jane's barn but he's not there all the time. He's a big ghost. He always wears a grey sweater. He smells like pipes. Sometimes he even smells like that pipe I found in the grass. I'm tired Mommy. Can you take me home now?"

CHAPTER SEVEN

"Mommy, there was a funny old lady at summer school today."

Gertrude slowed to turn into Jane's lane. The recent rain had left the puddles even deeper than they had been before. "Unh huh," said Gertrude paying more attention to where the puddles were than to what Roddy was saying.

Roddy tugged at her sleeve. "Mommy, listen to me. I have something 'portant to tell you."

Gertrude rolled to a stop in the dooryard and set the parking brake. She turned to Roddy. "So what's so important?"

"She was dressed in a very long dress and she was sort of fadey, like a ghost."

"Was she a visitor?" Gertrude watched Roderick's rosy face. "Did she say anything?"

"Not really. She was just there. When she started to fade more, she said something about a coat being in the parlour closet." Roddy stared down at his hands. "I don't think the others could see her because they were all working on their paintings. We were doing finger painting today, It was messy.

The teacher couldn't see her either, I don't think, because she scolded me for lollygagging. What's lollygagging, Mommy?"

"Wasting time," said Gertrude. She unbuckled Charlotte's car seat and lifted her carrier from the back seat, then hoisted the diaper bag onto her shoulder.

"But I wasn't wasting time, I'd already finished. The others take a lot longer than me, especially Jerry."

"Jerry can't work any faster, darling. He's handicapped." She fell silent for a few moments thinking over Roddy's news. "Is there anything else you can remember about the old lady?"

"She was pretty in an old kind of way. She smelled kind of pepperminty like the old ladies in church. She wasn't scary."

"That's good," said Gertrude. "Let's go inside now and see if Jane has any fresh cookies." She got out and unstrapped Roddy from his booster seat, then led the way indoors.

"You're here already," said Jane. "I barely had time to get started on 1905. It was odd though, it opened in February just about the time Julia showed up. I don't think Grandma was too pleased with her arrival. Grandma was all practised up to be the lead but when Julia arrived, she had to be just an understudy and a maid. She had some choice words to say about Julia."

"I wonder how they ever became friends?" said Gertrude. A tug at her elbow brought her attention to Roddy.

"I sure am hungry," said Roddy. "Did you say Jane might have a cookie?"

"I do, indeed," said Jane. "More than one too, and after that would you like to explore the cellar? I'll give you a lantern to light your way. It gets kind of dark in the corners down there."

"There's nothing down there that he can get into, is there?" asked Gertrude.

Jane shook her head. "Just some jam bottles and some wood for the stove. He'll be quite safe."

"The lantern?"

"It's battery," said Jane. "He'll be fine." She turned to Roddy. "D'you want a glass of milk to go with your cookie, Roddy?"

"Yes, please, and may I have two cookies?"

"You certainly may." Jane pulled a glass from the cupboard and filled it with milk and put two thick molasses cookies on a plate. She set the plate and the glass of milk in front of Roddy. "That glass was my favourite when I was a little girl. My grandma painted it. You'll see why it's so special in a moment."

"Manners, Roddy," said Gertrude.

"Thank you, Jane." Roddy took a bite of cookie

and a sip of milk. "This cookie tastes the way the old lady smelled today." His eyes grew as big as the plate of cookies. "D'you s'ppose she was here, Mommy?"

Gertrude shrugged. "Maybe. Old ladies seldom tell us where they're going. I remember asking my mother one time where she was going and she said: 'After my nose and my two big toes.' Eat your cookies so you can go exploring." She picked up the 1904 journal and began to leaf through it.

Roddy drank his milk and ate his cookies in record time. He slurped the last of his milk and said: "Ooh! What's that?"

"It's a cow," said Jane. "And if you look on the side of the glass you can see that her calf is looking for her and you just uncovered where she was hidden when you drank all your milk."

Roddy sat and puzzled over the cow and her calf for a moment or two. "But I just drank all the milk. What will the calf drink?"

Gertrude rolled her eyes. "Mommy cows always have milk for their babies. When it's all gone they just make more."

Roddy thought this over for a few minutes then muttered: "That's a good system," and climbed down from his chair. "I'm ready to go exploring now, Jane. Where's the lantern?"

"Right here." Jane turned the lantern on and

handed it to Roddy. "I'll have to open the hatch in the porch for you. It's pretty heavy."

Jane was back in a moment. "That was one excited little explorer. What was he saying about the old lady?"

"There was an old lady visited his playschool today, except I don't think she was real. I'll have to tell Don about this. I don't like this a bit. He'll be here at suppertime. From what Roddy said, she just faded from sight after she told him to look in the closet in the parlour. Is there something we missed in there?"

"Not that I know of," said Jane. "Lydia and I did a pretty thorough job of cleaning in there a few weeks ago, didn't we Lydia? There is no closet in the parlour. At least that I know about."

"Huh?" Lydia looked up from her reading. "This stuff is fascinating. Oh, hi, Gertrude. When did you arrive?"

"About fifteen minutes ago. You were very engrossed in your reading."

"As I said, this stuff is fascinating."

"Is that the 1905 journal?" asked Jane.

"Yes, it is. It's odd how friendships form in the theatre. Is that cookies I see?"

Jane passed her the tin of cookies. "So what's so fascinating?"

"Just the whole opera scene. She and Julia are

fast friends by the end of the journal. Grandma describes dresses and decorations and being backstage and all the gossip and what went on at rehearsals. She knew a lot of dirt on people."

"And she never told a soul," said Jane.

"She probably told your grandpa," said Gertrude.

"She probably did, but he'd never tattle either." Jane rummaged through the box and pulled out January 1904 to November 1904. "I wonder what's in here." She settled down to read.

"Here's the entry we're looking for," said Lydia. "It's February and Julia's just come to town. It seems that Grandma was completely blind-sided by this turn of events. It seems she wasn't expecting to be replaced at all."

"It's a wonder she didn't just withdraw altogether," said Jane

"She wanted to but she'd put so much effort into it by then she didn't want to give it up. She writes about all the things she'd like to do to Julia and the director, and actually plotted how to get back at them, Julia especially." Lydia flipped over a few pages. "Hm, that Julia must have been quite a charmer. Maybe Grandma was such a good actress that she made everyone think that it was okay with her."

"She was a professional and an actress, so maybe she did just cover it up," said Gertrude. "D'you suppose she stole Julia's coat and kept it hidden all these years."

"She could have done that," said Jane. "She could fib her way out of everything. Look at how she fooled the government men who came looking for 'shine."

"From what I've been reading I don't think she did," said Lydia. "Because when Julia came to town, she was lamenting the disappearance of this coat. So it had already gone missing."

A shriek sounded from the cellar. "Mommy! Mommy!" Gertrude was out of the kitchen and down the cellar stairs in a flash. "Where are you Roddy? Are you hurt?"

"I'm here, Mommy, I thought I saw the old lady again. I turned the light out so she'd disappear but she didn't. She had a lantern too. How did she know where I was?"

"Lucky guess," said Gertrude. "Turn your lantern back on so I can see you."

"I can't. I dropped it." Roddy began to cry. "Mommy, I'm scared."

"Can you see me?"

"No," Roddy wailed, "I've got my eyes closed."

Gertrude sighed. "Well, keep them closed while I go and get a flashlight."

Jane picked her way down the cellar steps with the light from a rather dim flashlight. "Take this and see if you can find the lantern. I'll stay here where I can still see the light from the porch."

Gertrude soon located a grubby Roddy. His face was streaked with tears and the red mud of the cellar. "You're a mess." She shone the flashlight around to see if she could see where the lantern had gotten to. "D'you know in which direction you threw it?"

"That way." Roddy pointed toward the corner by the boiler. "I threw it at her. She was standing right there." He turned and tried to hide his face in his mother's jeans. "I don't want to look anymore. She might still be there."

"She's not," said Gertrude, "and the next time I see her I'll tell her what I think of her antics."

"What's wrong with her attic, Mommy?"

"The word's antic. It means tricks and teasing. Jane's right over there. Can you see her? Go to her and she'll take you upstairs. I want to have a little look around."

"I can't see her, Mommy."

"Why can't you."

"I'm afraid to open my eyes." His voice wobbled

Gertrude sighed again. "There's nothing here anymore so you can open them."

Roddy peeked through half-closed eyes then made a run for Jane.

While Jane took Roddy upstairs, Gertrude began

to search for the lantern. She shone her meagre light in the direction that Roddy said he'd thrown it. At last she saw a glint of aluminum under the boiler. She fished it out and wiped the dirt off it with a tissue she had in her pocket. She looked under the boiler to see if there was anything else there. She saw nothing but the mellow gleam of copper farther on against the wall. She went around back and peered behind the boiler. Just a stack of old pipes, she thought. She turned to survey the rest of the clay cellar. Just cobwebs and red sandstone. I wonder why they would leave copper pipes like that. Maybe they're part of the still. Probably not though. If Grandpa was as smart as Jane says he was, he would have reused the pipes from that long ago. They must have been worth money even back then. She turned to go upstairs.

Back in the kitchen Roddy's cheeks were rosy. Jane had scrubbed most of the cellar dirt from his face and hands and taken the whisk broom to his trousers. He was somewhat presentable by the time Gertrude arrived.

"Roddy was just telling me about the lady in school today. D'you suppose it was Grandma?"

"From the description he gave me it was more likely Julia. Did your grandma eat peppermints?"

"Not often. They were too strong, she said." Jane rinsed the wash cloth free of red mud and hung it behind the stove to dry. "On the other hand, she once said that Julia was fond of them."

"So it must have been Julia who Roddy saw in his playroom."

"It would seem so." Jane sat down in the rocker and picked up the notebook for 1906.

Gertrude picked up a molasses cookie and began nibbling and thinking. She settled herself at the table. Presently she said: "Why would your grandfather have a stack of old copper pipe behind the boiler? Wouldn't it have been worth money to him?"

Jane marked her place on the page with a slender forefinger and looked up. "I don't know." She thought for a moment or two. "Y'know, I think you may have found part of his still!"

"D'you think so?" Gertrude thought about the possibility for a moment. "But why would he keep it back there?"

"Because he wanted it handy. The boiler that grandma said heated the household water wasn't a hot water heater originally. It was the body of the old still."

"Clever!" said Gertrude. "I wondered about that."

"Grandma warned me to never tell anyone about what was in the cellar. Just tell them, if strangers asked, that I never went down cellar, that I was afraid of spiders. She never said why I was afraid of spiders, but if she spoke in a particular tone of voice, I listened."

"So did anyone ever ask?"

"No, because when the government men came around I was always sent to my room and told to be very quiet and to not come down until they were gone. They were looking for stills long after Prohibition days."

"And where was your room?" Gertrude licked her finger and began dabbing at stray cookie crumbs.

"Right above here." Jane pointed to the hole in the ceiling above the stove. "There's a louvre on that, and if it was open, I could hear everything that was said in the kitchen."

"I'll bet you heard plenty, too."

Jane made a face. "More than the weather report." She bent her head to her journal again. After a few minutes she lifted her head. "D'you want to go down and see what's really behind the boiler?"

"Right now?"

"Why not? Roddy's taking a nap on the window seat. He'll sleep right through us going for a few minutes."

Gertrude looked over at her sleeping son. "You're probably right. Maybe we should go see what else is down there." She went over to the sink and picked up the dishcloth to wipe up the cookie crumbs that had escaped her finger's vigilance. "I'll just wipe up these before we go."

"I'll keep watch over Roddy," said Lydia. "You guys go exploring. I'm not too fond of spiders either." She returned to reading the journal she was working her way through.

Together Gertrude and Jane quietly lifted the cellar hatch again and climbed down the stone steps. "I'm glad you found the other flashlight," said Gertrude. "The one you had before was pretty dim."

"This is actually a trouble light. Grandpa was always in favour of things that did two jobs, so this you can detach from the power source and take with you. It runs quite awhile on stored energy." She shone the light around the periphery of the basement. "There's all kinds of things down here I never knew about."

"Look over there," said Gertrude. "What's behind that door?"

Jane shrugged. "I don't know. I didn't even know it was there before you pointed it out. I haven't been down here much, not even as a kid."

Gertrude chuckled. "Oh, yeah, you didn't like spiders." She headed over toward the door.

"No, I got locked down here once and no one knew I was here until suppertime. I wasn't strong enough to push the hatch open from this side and they couldn't hear me yelling. I was terrified. So

I haven't spent much time down here. Besides, I much preferred the barn and the barn loft."

"What was your reason for that?"

"They couldn't lock me in, and I had the animals to talk to." Jane jiggled the door handle on the door they'd just discovered. "Darn! It's locked."

"Is it really? Maybe it's just stuck." Gertrude tried the door knob too. It didn't move. "Maybe it's just rusted shut over the years."

"Perhaps if we put a little oil on it and let it sit awhile overnight," said Jane.

"Maybe it'll do the trick,"said Gertrude.

Jane gave the handle one last try with no luck. "There's no rush to get in there. I'll get Ian to come down here and do it for us the next time he's over. He'll know the right kind of oil to use."

After supper Don sat in the rocker playing horsey on his crossed leg with Roddy. "You'll be too big and heavy soon to do this," said Don.

"What'll we do then?" asked Roddy.

"Then it'll be Charlotte's turn. You're going to have to get off now, my leg is getting tired."

Gertrude sat at the table sipping tea and pondering the events of the afternoon. "I wonder if that's where the coat is."

Jane shrugged. "It's the only place we haven't looked."

Lydia looked up from her reading. "Maybe we should just call Ian to come over." She smiled at Jane. "He'd likely be here in a flash."

Jane sighed. She finished putting away the plates that Gertrude had dried then hung the dishtowel on the rack behind the stove. "Stop it, Lydia. Next thing you know you'll be letting something slip and embarrass both of us. Yourself too, likely."

"Uhn, uhn, not me." Lydia shook her head. "So, are you going to call him? If you don't, I will."

"Alright, I'll call him. Tomorrow."

"Tonight," said Lydia. She grinned at Jane and reached for the phone.

The crunch of gravel was heard through the open kitchen window. "I don't think you'll have to call," said Gertrude. "He just drove in."

"Good," said Jane. "Now I won't have to embarrass myself by calling him for no good reason."

"I think a stuck lock is as good a reason as any to call," said Lydia.

"Call who?" asked Ian. He shut the screen door behind himself.

"A locksmith," said Jane.

"You," said Lydia in unison with Jane.

"Hi, Ian," said Gertrude. Her eyes sparkled with mischief. "You're just in time to settle an argument. Lydia thinks Jane should call you to free up a lock. Jane doesn't want to bother you with every little thing."

"It's no bother, Jane," said Ian. He watched the pink creep into Jane's cheeks. "Where's the lock?"

"Down in the cellar. It's a padlock," said Jane. "It's the only place we haven't looked for that coat."

"The lock's probably rusty and just needs a little oil. I have some in my tool box. I'll just be a second." He headed back to his truck and rummaged in his toolbox in the back. In a moment he was back. "I brought bolt cutters too in case the oil doesn't work."

Jane stepped into the porch and unplugged the trouble light from its charger. Ian pulled open the cellar hatch and together they made their way down.

"It's darker in here than it was this afternoon."

"The sun has almost set," said Ian. He took the trouble light from Jane and held it higher. "What were you doing down here this afternoon? There's nothing down here except cobwebs."

"I sent Roddy down here to explore, and he said he saw an old lady down here, and he threw his light at her and screamed. Of course, we all came running. Gertrude got to him first because I stopped long enough to grab the light. Gertrude quieted him and sent him upstairs with me. Gertrude found some pipes behind the boiler. I came back and we found the door that I didn't even know was here. It was locked so we couldn't open it, hence the discussion about who to call." Jane paused for breath.

Ian took her by the shoulders and turned her to face him. "Jane, you don't need to call anybody to do the odd job around here. I'm always happy to come by. Besides, you make good cookies." He released her and shone the light on the lock. He tried it but it wouldn't work. "You're right, it's rusted pretty solid." He squirted some oil into the key hole. "That should help. We'll let 'er sit for a bit. If that doesn't work I can always cut the bolt if you don't mind."

"I don't mind," said Jane. "The sooner we get to the bottom of the coat mystery, the sooner I can sleep soundly at night. There are too many secrets in this house." Jane turned abruptly to head for the stairs but ran into Ian's solid bulk in the semi-darkness. She overbalanced and Ian grabbed her to keep her from falling altogether. He held her snugly until she had seemed to regain her balance. She stayed within the secure circle of his arms for a moment longer, then peeked up at him silhouetted by the feeble light of the trouble light. He bent his head and kissed her gently on the cheek, then on the lips. She sighed and kissed him back.

"We're going to have to stop meeting like this,"

he whispered. A small chuckle escaped his lips at the ideas engendered by the cliche.

Jane stayed in his arms for a brief moment longer. "I agree," she whispered back.

Ian turned and tried the lock one more time before they went upstairs. It gave a little. He applied more oil. "That should get that moving pretty soon." He wiggled the key again. "Maybe I'll check it one more time before I leave this evening." He looked across at Jane.

"Maybe you will." Her voice sounded sleepy.

"You know, you don't have to hesitate to call me for any little thing."

"I know that. Now."

"You'll be staying for tea, Ian?" Gertrude asked.

Ian looked at Jane.

"Of course you're staying," said Jane. "I'll just fill the kettle."

"Already have," said Gertrude.

"Oh! Oh!" said Lydia excitedly. "I think I found the reason why Grandma didn't like Julia." She jumped to her feet and began pacing. "I'll bet that's the reason why. Listen here, you guys. This is what she says about Julia when she arrives." She began to read. "'Our new leading lady arrived this evening. Our director told me that she was just in from

Paris and we were lucky to get her. Never a word nor a thank you about all my hard work. Not only that but she was late besides. I looked around at the others and you could have knocked the men's eyes off with sticks. She is pretty but not nearly as much as she thinks she is. She'd better leave Angus alone or she'll have me to deal with.'"

"Wow! I wonder how that played out? How did she and Grandma get to be such good friends?" said Gertrude. "I wish Mary Ann would get here. I'm eager to get started this evening."

"I thought Julia doesn't like Mary Ann," said Lydia.

"Too bad," said Gertrude. A crash came from the parlour. Everyone startled and Roddy woke up with a shriek.

"Mommy! Mommy! That lady is here again, isn't she?"

Gertrude sat down beside Roddy on the window seat and brushed the sleep damp hair from his forehead. "It seems as if she is. I guess she didn't like what I said about it being too bad about what she likes and doesn't like."

"You didn't say very much," said Lydia.

"No, but she's a diva and thinks it's all about her and what she wants."

"She must be here more than we realize," said Jane. "Else how could she have heard us talking?"

"I don't know how much she hangs around listening," said Gertrude. "I don't even know if there's a way to find out."

"Is there any way to stop her?" asked Jane.

"Find her coat," said Gertrude.

"Wherever that is," said Lydia.

Mary Ann bumped and splashed her way down the lane. She peeled her plump self out of her red Morris Mini. It was coated in mud, and water dripped from the bumpers from the trip down the lane. Gertrude greeted her at the door.

"I need a bigger car," said Mary Ann. "This one seems so much smaller than when I bought it." She straightened her cardigan more comfortably around her hips.

Gertrude's lips twitched. "I don't suppose it has anything to do with cookies?"

Mary Ann made a face.

"I was blaming it on shrinkage. We've had so much rain lately."

"That must be it," said Gertrude. She managed to keep a straight face.

"So, what's up for this evening?"

"We need to have more specific directions for finding the coat," said Gertrude. "Julia is becoming a nuisance. She's been terrorizing Roddy all day."

"How so?" asked Mary Ann.

"She followed him to school and then back here this afternoon. Poor Roddy was in great distress earlier." Gertrude told Mary Ann about Roddy's adventures of the day.

"Nasty old busybody," said Mary Ann. "I'm glad she's long gone." The teacup that held the last sips of Mary Ann's supper tea twisted out of her hands and flew across the room striking the storage tins of sugar and flour, knocking them onto the floor. Everyone startled. "Like I said, nasty old woman."

"What a mess!" said Jane. She went to fetch the broom and dustpan.

"What a waste!" said Lydia. "I just filled those today."

"Julia, there was no call for that!" said Gertrude. "Settle down, or I'll stop looking for your coat."

A low moan of sadness echoed through the house.

"I guess she heard me," said Gertrude. "It would really help if she'd be more explicit so we could find the coat and just give it back to her."

"We need to get better answers from her," said Mary Ann. "Are you going to trance this evening or am I? Maybe both of us? Can Molly help us?"

"I'm sorry Mary Ann, I told you last week, she doesn't want to work with you. I didn't know how to tell you without hurting your feelings."

"Why? How d'you know that?"

"She told me. She said she didn't like you. She said you are distracting. I just know that she's never as forthcoming when you trance with me. As for Molly helping us. I don't know. She doesn't seem to be in a helping mood lately."

Mary Ann let a little puff of air escape through her lips in exasperation. "Fired by a ghost!" She sat thinking this over for a few moments. "Then I'll stay awake and just watch over you."

"That's fine with me. I don't altogether trust her," said Gertrude. "You don't mind tending the children do you, Don?"

"I never have before," said Don. He smiled across at Gertrude. "I even packed the diaper bag before I left."

"You two go ahead," said Jane. "I'm almost finished here." She dried the last plate and put the stack away in the cupboard, then wrung out the dishcloth and hung it and the dishtowel behind the stove to dry. The water disappeared down the drain and she rinsed the sink free of soap residue. "There, I'm done. The parlour is all yours. We'll be as quiet as mice here. Charlotte is sleeping like an angel in her carrier so you don't have to worry about that."

Gertrude and Mary Ann scraped back their chairs and headed for the parlour. Gertrude settled herself into Grandpa's old easy chair and Mary Ann sat on the chair in the corner. "Where's Jim this evening?"

"He decided to stay home. He's working on some house plan or other of some haunting out in Lyndale. He said he didn't need to be here, that you can handle it."

"I think I might need a blanket," said Gertrude. "It's quite chilly in here this evening."

Mary Ann pulled the afghan off the settee and tucked Gertrude into it. "Maybe it's just the ghosties. They always like to play it cool."

"Um, hm," muttered Gertrude, her voice already muffled and sleepy. Her eyes closed and the room became colder still. Mary Ann huddled in the corner armchair. "I wish I'd brought my sweater in," she muttered.

Gertrude began to mumble. "It's where? But we all looked there already."

"Freddie said it was in the parlour, and that's all she'll say. I think she had a mean streak."

"We're reading as fast as we can. There are about twenty-five or thirty notebooks and Grandma's handwriting is not the easiest to read." She sighed. "We'll keep looking." Gertrude was silent for a long minute or two. "Why is the coat so important?"

"Oh, I see. Which lover? Mr. Argent. I see." Gertrude sighed and stirred. "Julia, please don't be scaring Roddy. He's only a little boy yet." She opened her eyes and stared sleepily around the room. She turned and saw Mary Ann asleep in the armchair. "Watching over me indeed!" she muttered. She threw the afghan off and headed for the kitchen waking Mary Ann as she went by.

Roddy was in an agitated state when she opened the door. He ran to her and hugged her around the waist. It was as high as he could reach.

"What's the matter, Roddy?" Gertrude peeled him off her body.

"I was afraid that old lady had taken you away. I got so cold. Is she bad?"

Gertrude sat down on the window seat and pulled Roddy onto her lap. "No, darling, she's not bad. She's just an old lady who's lost her coat. And anyway, she can't take me away. I'm here with you and the only way she can talk to me is in my mind and only if I concentrate. You'll be able to do that too when you're older."

"I hope he's lots older before he starts that stuff," said Don. "I was worried about you too, Gertrude. It got so cold in here, and I know it's not the weather."

"I thought we'd been all over this years ago. You know I can't actually get hurt. Those on the other side can't hurt us here."

"If you'd been in the path of that flying teacup earlier, I'd say you could have been plenty hurt."

Gertrude sighed. "I'd know enough to duck." She sat stroking Roddy's silky red hair until she felt the tension leave his body. After a few minutes he scrambled down from her lap.

"So what did you find out?" asked Jane. She rubbed her arms to warm them.

"She's definitely looking for her coat. She says we can find the answer in the journals and that the coat is in the parlour. There's no coat there, not even a closet. I don't know what she's talking about."

A sigh whispered through the kitchen.

"Wow!" said Lydia. "She must think we're awfully dense. That sigh nearly blew us away."

"The only think I can think to do is to keep reading the journals. She said the answer is there."

"I'm doing my best," said Lydia. "I'm halfway through the fifth one. I haven't come across anything useful yet."

"I'm reading from the other end of the stack and I haven't found anything either," said Jane. She reached for her sweater behind the stove and slipped her still chilly arms into it. "Does anyone mind if I add another stick to the fire? I'm still cold."

"Go ahead," said Gertrude. "Trancing is never very warm work, and if you guys were affected here, Julia must be working with a lot of energy."

"I must go home," said Ian. "I have to feed Cedric and the chickens and close things up for the night. Walk me to the truck, Jane."

They walked hand in hand to Ian's truck. Cedric

was asleep on the seat. He lifted his head and whined when Ian opened the door.

"Out you get, then, Cedric," said Ian. "Go water some plants"

Jane laughed. "You must speak 'Cedric.'"

"By now I know most of what his grunts and whines are all about. He's also put out that I left him in the truck by himself."

"Why didn't you bring him in?"

"Because he's decided that he doesn't want to come in."

"Charlie doesn't like coming any farther than the porch these days either."

"Maybe after Julia gets her coat the house will quiet down enough so those two won't mind coming in anymore." Ian took Jane's hand again and pulled her into the shelter of his arms. Together they stood quietly waiting for Cedric's return.

"He's taking a long time," said Jane. She stirred in Ian's arms.

"Let him," said Ian. He pulled Jane closer still and kissed her. She sighed and kissed him back.

"Are we going anywhere with this?" asked Ian. "I'm getting too old to be playing teeny bopper games."

"I hope so," Jane whispered. "I've never felt so right with anyone before. There was always something missing." She was silent for a long moment.

"Come to think of it, I've felt this way since I was a little girl. Since I painted the fence and you took me to the stream to wash off."

Ian laughed. "That was a long time ago."

Just then Cedric came bounding out of the shadows and stretched up Ian's leg for an ear scratch. Ian opened the door for him. "Get in, you furry creature. We'll go home in a minute." He closed the door and the dome light shut off. They stood together in the late dusk for a moment longer. "I'll be by tomorrow to check that lock."

"Come for breakfast?"

"I don't think so. Everything is too new for people to speculate, even our best friends."

Jane laughed. "Too late for that. Lydia has been match making for weeks. I don't discuss my business with anyone, not even her. As you said, we're not teenagers anymore."

"Found it!" Lydia almost jumped out of her rocking chair in her excitement. They had been up until well past midnight the night before trying to decipher Grandma's spidery writing, and they had started in again right after breakfast.

"What did you find?" Jane looked over at Lydia. Her eyes darkened with hope.

"I think I've found the clue to where the coat

is." Lydia shoved the notebook in Jane's direction.

Jane set her notebook aside and took the one Lydia was waving toward her and trying to point out the passage at the same time. She searched the thin text. "I don't see what you mean." She reread the two pages.

"There. Halfway down the first page."

Jane looked again. "All I see is a passage about Grandpa refacing the old fireplace. There's nothing about that fireplace that is out of the ordinary. I think that all they did was cover up the old crumbly bricks and put a wooden surround on it. Grandma said something about it once. I didn't take much note."

"But don't you see? That's the one place in the parlour that we didn't look. We didn't look behind the fireplace."

"But there's nothing behind the fireplace except perhaps some remnants of old book cases. But I don't think there's even that because Grandpa was very aware of fireplaces and the possibility of fires. Anyway, if Grandma had a beautiful coat like that why would she hide it?"

"Who knows? I'm beginning to think your ancestors were a little bit squirrely."

"I know they were unique, but squirrely? C'mon."

"Nevertheless ..." said Lydia.

"Look, we can solve this by just checking out

the fireplace." Jane jumped to her feet and headed toward the parlour. "Are you coming?"

"I don't like the parlour. You go."

"Oh, for heaven's sake! There's nothing in the parlour."

Lydia followed Jane into the parlour but stayed at running range of the door. Jane began examining the fireplace surround, tapping here and tapping there and running her fingers along the edges. The fireplace surround was just what it seemed and apparently nothing more.

Lydia abandoned her post by the door. "I think I just heard something. A click or a clunk?"

"Anybody home this morning?" Ian's voice sounded from the kitchen.

Jane and Lydia startled. They abandoned their search and joined Ian in the kitchen. "We're both here," said Jane. "Lydia thought she read something in one of Grandma's journals about the fireplace being a hiding place so we were just checking it out."

"I doubt there's anything there," said Ian. "My father helped your grandfather build that surround when he was just a lad. I think he might have said something about any irregularities in its construction but there was never a whisper. Of course, maybe he just kept it to himself. He was just as secretive as the rest of them." A loud sigh issued from the parlour.

"Poor Julia must think we're awfully dense," said Lydia.

"We are," said Jane, "according to her point of view."

Ian pulled out a chair at the kitchen table and sat down. "Is there any coffee on the go?"

"Just instant," said Jane. "Grandma didn't have a coffee maker except that old beat-up one that was missing its lid. I think she used it for watering her plants at the end."

"That'd be your Grandma. Waste not, want not. Instant is fine. I need a little pick-me-up about now. I had a calf come early, last night. The cow was a new mother and couldn't quite get the hang of looking after a newborn. She had me up half the night."

"You do look tired," said Jane. She pulled the kettle over the hot part of the stove and it was soon bubbling. She pulled out mugs still warm from being washed after breakfast and set them on the table. "Did you get anything to eat yet this morning?"

"I made toast and a couple of eggs before I milked and let the cows out to pasture. The calves are on grass now and almost ready for sale. Some of them will be good milkers when they're old enough."

"What about the one that calved last night?"

"She got loose after all the other cows had been bred. She was only young. I wouldn't have bred her for another year. She got with Jack's bull before I could round her up again."

"Naughty girl," said Jane.

"You didn't even have time to have a fatherly chat with her?" said Lydia.

"Alas, no," said Ian. "I doubt she'd have the wits to listen anyway."

Jane set a mug of coffee on the table in front of Ian. Lydia pushed the cream and sugar closer to him then sat down opposite him.

"Show me the entry in the journal. Perhaps it'll jog my memory," said Ian. He stirred his coffee then licked the spoon.

Jane handed him the appropriate notebook opened to the page. Ian perused it carefully then turned to the entries before and after. "Grandma was keen on weather reports, wasn't she?"

"Their lives revolved around them even after they stopped farming."

"Dad's too," said Ian. "He didn't keep a journal, he just kept notes on the latest calendar and then saved them. His own father did it before him. They're mildly interesting to read." He sipped his coffee in silence for a moment or two. He pursed his lips. "He did note some rod or other he had gotten for Angus and brought it over here.

"Could it have been a closet rod?" asked Lydia.

"I don't think so, it was pretty short, if it was as

short as he wrote down."

"Could it have been something to do with his moonshine business?" asked Jane.

"Perhaps. Come to think about it. Dad did like a little sip on the sly. Mom was adamantly against it, but Dad wasn't. She wouldn't allow it in the house." He sipped his coffee. "Did you ever get that door in the cellar opened?"

"No, I kind of forgot about it. I really haven't been down there since. I seldom have reason to go."

"It's kind of a job for a rainy day, don't you think." Ian drained his cup then rose from his chair. "I have to get back. I don't know if that cow will know enough to let her calf nurse without help and it's two hours since she was fed."

"Come back for supper?" asked Jane.

Chapter Eight

The back door slapped on its hinges and Ian came into Jane's kitchen.

"Dinner's not quite ready yet," said Jane. She gave the gravy another stir to keep it from sticking then stuck a fork into the new potatoes to test for doneness.

"I brought my trouble light and the long extension cord in case we need a second light." He waved the items in the air. "Also the bolt cutters and a new lock."

"Wow!" said Jane, "you came prepared."

"As Dad used to say, 'a workman is worthy of his hire.'"

Jane peeled off the apron she was wearing and hung it over the back of the nearest chair. "Lydia, will you mind the supper while we go treasure hunting? Make sure the gravy doesn't solidify."

Lydia lifted her head from the journal she was reading. "Huh?"

"Nothing, just don't let the supper burn."

"Um, I won't." She returned to her reading.

Jane and Ian made their way down the steep

stone steps into the cellar. "I hope she doesn't," said Jane. "The gravy is just right now." Together they made their way across to the locked door.

Ian hung his trouble light from a convenient hook in the floor joist above. His bolt cutters made quick work of the padlock. He lifted the latch and pushed the door. It was very stiff on its hinges. The scurry of rodent feet whispered in the stale air that whooshed out as Ian applied his sturdy shoulder to widen the door.

"What's in there?" Jane had been holding her breath in her excitement and could only whisper.

"Hand me the light," said Ian. "This door is so badly hung that it'll shut if I let go."

Jane lifted the light from its hook and handed it to Ian.

Ian held the light high for maximum illumination. "I think we've found Grandpa's still." Ian echoed Jane's whisper.

"Why are we whispering?" asked Jane.

"I dunno. You were, so I thought I'd better too."

Jane peered around the edge of the rough door frame. "I was holding my breath in excitement."

"Is there anything handy that I can prop this door open with?"

Jane handed him a brick left over from when the chimney was built.

"Where are we in relation to the other rooms

upstairs?" Ian pushed the brick hard into the dirt so it wouldn't slip.

Jane lifted the light higher. "I think we're under the parlour or very close to it." She moved the light around the walls of the room. "There! I think that's the base of the fireplace and the flue to the kitchen stove." Her voice rose to a squeak. She looked more closely. "It's awfully narrow, though."

Ian climbed over the debris of decades and began patting and knocking around the brickwork. "It's definitely the chimney, I can feel the heat from the stove."

"No wonder the mice like it in here."

"They must have a way in."

"This house is likely full of mouse doors around the foundation," said Jane. "I'll have to get a cat."

"Missy just had a litter of kittens. In a few weeks they'll be big enough to give you one."

"Not until after their mother teaches them to hunt or they'll be no good to me." Jane turned toward the door. The light illuminated the corner behind the door. "What's that over there?" Jane scrambled over a pile of discarded building supplies. "It's a chest." She crept nearer in the light cast by the trouble light. "I think that's Grandpa's old tool chest. I wonder what's in it?"

"Tools, probably," said Ian. "Why don't you open it?" He joined Jane on the other side of the rubble heap.

Jane gave a heave to the heavy lid. It didn't budge. "It's stuck. Give me a hand."

Together they tried to lift the tight lid.

"I wonder what's holding it?" said Ian. "Hang on a second. I'll get the light." He clambered back to where he'd hung the light and handed it to Jane, then clambered back to her side. "Shine the light here."

Jane swung the light to illuminate the front of the chest. "It's locked! No wonder we couldn't get it open."

"I'll get my bolt cutters," said Ian. He retrieved his bolt cutters and with some effort managed to cut through the heavy lock. Together they lifted the lid.

"It's full of old bank notes," said Jane. "This must be where he kept his money. Mom once said that he didn't trust banks."

"There seems to be an awful lot of them here. I wonder how much they're worth in today's currency?"

"Why don't we take one to the bank and see if anyone knows," said Jane. She peeled off a fifty dollar bill and stuck it in her jeans pocket. "We'd better shine the light around here and see if there's anything else of value that's hiding in the shadows."

"Like a fur coat?" asked Ian.

"Just like that,"said Jane. She let the lid of the chest drop and turned to clamber over the pile of dirt.

Ian grabbed her arm and turned her to face him. "Have you thought any more about what we were talking about the other evening?"

"Jane, Ian, supper's on the table." Lydia's voice sounded far away in the sudden rush of blood in Jane's ears.

"Coming, Lydia."

Ian pulled Jane into a quick hug. "I guess you'll have to think a little longer." He kissed her gently on the cheek, then let her go.

Together they climbed the stairs.

"You've got spiderwebs in your hair," said Ian. He brushed gently at the dust that had accumulated on Jane's crown.

"Just as long as there are no spiders," said Jane. Her voice still quavered a little at Ian's caress.

"Jane ... " Ian began.

"We'll be going back to school next week and Lydia'll only be here on weekends." Jane gave Ian's hand a quick squeeze, then took a deep breath. "Soon."

"Until next week, then," said Ian. They went into the kitchen.

"Gertrude should be here this evening. We can tell her what we've discovered," said Jane.

"What did you discover?" asked Lydia.

"The base of the chimney and Grandpa's old still, and a chest full of treasure," said Jane.

"G'way with you," said Lydia. "Treasure?"

Jane pulled the old bill from her pocket. "Yeah, a whole chest full of bills just like this one as well as hundred dollar bills. Ian and I are going to take it to the bank tomorrow to see if it's redeemable."

"Wow," said Lydia. "I hope for your sake it is." She stared at the old bill. "The date on this says 1930."

"That's when he sold all the foxes and shut down the business," said Jane.

"At least we know now what he did with the still and all his money. What's so important about the base of the chimney?"

"I can see you're not as excited as we were to open that door," said Ian.

"I've been wading through the journals all afternoon," said Lydia. "They were pretty boring. Excuse me if I can't dredge up much enthusiasm just now. I'm practically cross-eyed from reading Grandma's spidery handwriting."

"You'll survive," said Jane. She tied the apron back on and began to put food into serving bowls. "Thanks for minding the supper for us. Plates in the warming oven?"

Lydia nodded.

"Is Cedric with you this evening?" asked Jane. She began filling water glasses and setting them at each place.

"He's tethered in the barn with Charlie. I didn't know if the ghosts would be here right now or not. He doesn't seem to mind the energy in there."

"Good idea. I put Charlie in there just before you came."

"What time are you expecting Gertrude?" asked Ian. He slid into his seat at the table.

"About seven. Don said he'd mind the kids this evening so she'll get them ready for bed before she comes, then he can tuck them in later." Jane and Lydia took their places as well.

"So it'll just be Gertrude this evening? No Mary Ann?"

"She may come but Gertrude said that Julia doesn't like her much for some reason. She sometimes watches over Gertrude while she's in trance," said Jane. "Apparently it takes a lot of energy from Gertrude to work like that. I don't know that much about the process so I can't say. I've never actually seen her in trance." Jane passed the yellow beans to Lydia. "I'm so glad you put the garden in this spring Ian, even though Grandma thought she'd be coming home to tend it and you figured she wouldn't."

He smiled across at Jane, then accepted the bowl

of vegetables from Lydia. "So, Lydia, are you looking forward to getting back in the classroom?" he asked. He filled the remainder of his plate with vegetables fresh from the garden only an hour ago.

"Oh, yes, I always do," said Lydia. "That age group are always interesting. They'll have so many stories to tell about what they did all summer."

"Will you tell them yours?" asked Jane.

"Maybe at Hallowe'en. I just hope the story is completed before then. I don't think the parents will like it if I tell it for truth, though."

"Probably not," said Jane. "If it hadn't happened to me, I wouldn't have believed it at all."

Supper was soon over and the dishes nearly done when Gertrude arrived. "You can really tell it's nearly fall out there," she said. "The days are noticeably shorter." She hung her jacket on the hook behind the stove. "It'll be cool going home."

"Don is minding the kids?" asked Lydia.

"He has the whole evening planned. He and Roddy are going to watch a kiddy cartoon and eat popcorn. Charlotte is already in bed. Roddy is allowed to stay up past his bedtime to watch the movie but he promised to go to bed right after."

"He's pretty obedient, isn't he?" said Jane. She gave a final wipe to the counter and hung the dishcloth over the water spout in the sink to dry.

"Most of the time," said Gertrude. "We reminded him this evening that school was starting next week and he won't be able to stay up past his bedtime after that."

"What did he say to that?" asked Ian.

"He just said: 'I know, Mommy. I have to have a proper sleep so I can learn better.' Then he said: 'If I get into my pyjamas before Daddy and I watch the movie can I stay 'til the end?'"

Ian laughed. "He's got it all figured out."

"What have you guys been doing?" asked Gertrude.

"We got the door downstairs open this evening and found Grandpa's still, or at least more parts of it. A chest full of money and a lot of mice."

"A lot of money!" Gertrude almost shrieked. "Wow! Where did that come from?"

"We think it must have been the proceeds from the fox farm," said Jane. "He didn't trust banks or the stock market. The chest is full of it."

"Have you counted it yet?"

"Not yet," said Jane. "We only just found it a few hours ago. I think I should leave it where it is until I can get it evaluated by the bank. It was under two padlocks. Ian had to cut them off. Please don't say anything about it outside of this room."

"You never know how many greedy crazies are out there," said Gertrude. "Don't worry, my lips are sealed until you reveal it first. I can tell Don, can't I?"

"Of course, but no one else,"said Jane.

"What else have you been doing?" asked Gertrude.

"We've been wading through Grandma's diaries," said Jane.

"It's a monumental task," grumbled Lydia. "She had an awful lot to say about everything and everyone. Something I've been wondering, did Grandpa have a fling with Julia while she was here? "

"I've never heard so much as a whisper on that subject but it's not impossible. It would give us the answer to some of our questions about why she didn't like Julia much except they were supposedly best friends back then."

"Yeah, but don't forget Grandma was an actress. And from the sound of these stories she read people extremely well. She could lead them down the garden path quite easily and they'd never even guess."

"She was pretty accurate, though," said Jane. "I was only a child and I can still recognize some of the people who came here. Of course, now they're all dead."

"I read an entry where you helped her weed the garden," said Lydia. "Grandpa was in the barn talking to some guy from the government about who had stills around yet, so she was keeping you out of the way."

"I think I remember that day," said Jane. "Grandpa was being particularly charming and smooth and I wondered why."

"Any more activity in the house?" asked Gertrude.

"No, but Charlie still won't come in so I'm assuming that Julia, at least, must be around."

Just then one of the crystal bells in Grandma's china cabinet in the parlour tinkled. "I guess we have our answer," said Gertrude. In the barn Charlie and Cedric howled in unison. "Someone's definitely here. I guess I'd better go and see what I can find out this evening."

She rose from her seat and made her way to the parlour. Her eyes were already feeling heavy. She pulled the afghan from the sofa and wrapped up in it before making herself comfortable in her usual chair. I wish Mary Ann were here, she thought then lapsed into trance.

"Took you long enough." Julia's form gradually materialized in Gertrude's inner vision.

"I do have children," said Gertrude. Her tone was a little stern.

"I know and it makes me glad I didn't," said Julia. Her colours started to deepen as her energy got stronger. "I see they've found the still. They can't be far from the coat now." Her voice sounded far away. "Freddie said to look for a ring."

"What kind of ring?" asked Gertrude. "A wedding ring? A key ring?"

"Look up, she said," said Julia. After her initial spate of energy she began to fade. "She said it's right in front of your eyes." Her voice became fainter.

"That's not an answer," muttered Gertrude. "Come back here and tell me properly." But Julia had gone. Gertrude felt the trance lifting and did not have the psychic energy to sustain it. She yawned and stretched, then rose and folded the afghan and put it back on the sofa. That wasn't a whole lot of help, she thought. I wish Mary Ann were here. Julia doesn't like her for some reason, but she does add to the energy. Gertrude made her way to the kitchen.

"You weren't long," said Jane.

"No, she didn't seem to want to hang around this evening. Her energy started out strong but it faded quickly and I didn't have enough to keep her there."

"Did she tell you anything useful?" asked Lydia.

"I don't know how useful it is, but she told me that Grandma said to look for a ring. She said to look up, that it was right in front of me, whatever she meant by that. Does it mean anything to you, Jane?"

"Not off-hand. Where were you sitting?"

"In Grandpa's chair opposite the fireplace."

"The only thing that would have been in front of you would have been that portrait of Great-grandfather. I don't think I recall a ring connected with that," said Jane.

"Is there anything unusual about that portrait?"

Jane shrugged. "Nothing that I would say was out of the ordinary. It's a formal painting. It's been there ever since I can remember."

"Maybe we should go and have a closer look at it," said Lydia.

"Don't go in there without me," said Ian. He rose from his chair. "I have to feed the dogs. I'll only be a minute." In the barn the two dogs howled in unison.

"We've got a bass and a tenor," said Lydia. "I wonder if we could find an alto and a soprano somewhere?"

Ian was back in five minutes."The dogs are really reacting to the energy this evening. They're huddled together under a pile of straw and wouldn't come out, not even for dinner."

"This place really has Charlie spooked."

"He'll probably be glad to go home next week," said Jane. "Not that I'm eager to get rid of you guys but he really doesn't like it here, does he?"

Lydia's glance slid over to Ian and back again. "You'll be by yourself. You'll need to get a dog just for the company."

Ian cleared his throat. "Let's go see what that

portrait can tell us."

In the parlour the air was very dense and oppressive. "Phew!" said Gertrude. "It's a lot heavier in here than it was awhile ago. Something must be up. How long has it been since that portrait has been up there without being moved?"

"I don't know if it ever was moved," said Jane. "Certainly not when I was around. I can remember Grandma dusting it with a long-handled duster but I've never seen it anywhere but on the wall."

"Hm," said Gertrude. "Maybe we should just stand back and look at it to see if there's anything in the portrait that we wouldn't see if we didn't look for it. Turn the ceiling light on."

The dim bulb in the ceiling light did little but cast shadows and confuse the image. They all squinted at the portrait and looked at it from every angle possible. "Stupid!" echoed in Gertrude's mind.

"I am not," said Gertrude. "You're obscure!" She continued to stare at the painting. The collective effort of the group made the portrait swing on its wire holder and suddenly the whole portrait let go and fell with a crash.

"Now do you see it?" The question resounded in Gertrude's mind.

Gertrude blinked and stood staring at the place where the portrait had hung. She was almost in full trance just staring at the blank wall. She had a muttered conversation with someone whom only she could see. The others just stood gaping at her.

"Oh, for heaven's sake, Freddie," she muttered. Then she gasped. "I see it now. It's not in the painting, it's on the wall."

"Took you long enough," said Freddie. "Now push the centre."

Gertrude went closer and inspected the decorative circle that had been hidden behind the portrait. She reached up and gently rubbed the centre. Nothing happened.

"For goodness sake, Gertrude, push it harder." Freddie's voice echoed in the parlour.

Everyone startled except Gertrude. She reached up and pushed hard. The surround of the fireplace swung open revealing the old stone fireplace underneath. The mantle shelf wobbled on its supports. Ian grabbed it to keep it from falling. His grab dislodged the surround further and a space could be seen beside the old fireplace. "Give me a hand with this," he said. He lifted the surround off its makeshift hinges. The spigot for the old still fell off a concealed shelf. They propped the surround on the far wall.

Jane inspected the shelf for whatever else it might be holding. "Hand me a flashlight," she said. "It's as dark as Egypt in here and dusty." She poked around on the shelf. "A photograph album," she exclaimed. "I wonder why this is in here?" She handed it out to Lydia. "I don't see anything else, it's too dark." She swung her flashlight into the recess below the shelf. At the back on a hook there was a garment. "I think we've found that wretched coat." She stepped back and handed the flashlight to Ian. "Here, I can't reach it, maybe you can, your arms are longer."

"I also don't mind spiders," said Ian. He reached into the space and brought forth a garment bag. It had a zipper on the front but sticking up at the hangar hook was a tuft of silvery grey hair.

Jane unzipped the garment bag with unsteady hands. The bag opened to a beautiful fox fur coat and a set of pearls. "Wow!" She stared at the contents of the garment bag. "It's no wonder she wants her coat. This is gorgeous. I doubt there's anything like it around here these days."

"You'll have to try it on," said Lydia. "It might fit you."

"Where am I going to wear such a thing."

"No!" Gertrude was still in trance. "It's mine. I want it back."

"What?" Jane said.

Gertrude came out of the depths of her mind to a shallower level. "Julia and Freddie are both here and Julia wants her coat back. I have to give it to her. Take a picture of it and give it back." She lapsed back into deep trance again.

Jane grabbed her camera and took a picture. "I hope this turns out," she said.

Gertrude began muttering from her seat in Grandpa's chair. "Give it to me," she muttered. "Give it to me."

"Does she mean physically give it to her?" said Lydia.

"Give it to me!" Gertrude was becoming more insistent.

"I guess she does," said Jane. She picked up the coat and handed it to Gertrude. It held the faint hint of ancient perfume. Lavender.

Gertrude held it on her lap for a moment stroking the softness of it. A glow began to gather around the coat and then in a moment the coat seemed to dissolve like morning mist in the sun. In a moment it was gone. Gertrude sat and continued to stroke the air where it had been. "Beautiful," she muttered. "Goodbye, Julia," she mumbled. "It has been nice knowing you." She relaxed into the armchair and stopped stroking the air. "After a few moments she stirred and opened her eyes. "Did you find it?" she asked.

"Don't you know?" asked Jane.

"I was too deeply in trance to know anything that happened here," said Gertrude. She blinked and shook her head as if to clear it. "All I know is that I handed a fur coat to Julia and she was very happy. So I guess you must have found it."

"We did and it's gone," said Jane. "I didn't even get to try it on."

"You got a picture of it," said Lydia.

"I hope those two pictures turn out," said Jane, "otherwise no one will believe us."

"We will," said the other three in unison.

Several days later the ghost hunters gathered in the parlour for a celebratory *ceildh*. "So big school opens this week, Roddy. What do you think of that?" asked Jim. For once he had set aside his research project to join the others.

"It will be nice to see all my winter time friends again," said Roddy. His voice was prim as if every adult he met asked him that and he was becoming rote about the answer.

"What about your summer time friends? Won't you miss them?

"Not really. Some of those go to my school so I'll see them often."

"I see Charlie and Cedric have joined us this evening," said Mary Ann. She helped herself to a few chips and dip. "What brought them indoors finally?"

"I don't know," said Lydia. "Charlie just showed up on the doorstep the next day scratching to be let in."

"I thought you kept him tied," said Don.

"He managed to get free and he appeared there with his chain dragging behind him. He didn't seem to notice."

"And Cedric?"

Ian shook his head. "I dunno. It seems where Charlie goes Cedric is willing to follow."

"Look what I found!" Jane's voice held great excitement as she came into the parlour. She was carrying a tray loaded with an old fashioned bottle with a cork in it. The cork had been waxed in place. A set of grandma's glasses tinkled on the tray beside it.

"Where'd you get that?" asked Lydia.

"What is it?" wondered Mary Ann.

"I found it in the room in the basement this afternoon," said Jane. "I think it's the last bottle of Grandpa's rum."

"Wow!" said Ian. "I've seen bottles like that at my house when I was little. I always just thought it was cough medicine. Dad used to have a little glass for his chest, as he called it. Mom always looked at him with pursed lips when he'd have some. Once I saw him coming back from visiting your grandfather carrying a bottle just like that. Once I got older I just forgot about it, and then Dad started getting his 'cough syrup' from town, then after awhile he stopped altogether. I think my mother had a hand in that."

"Well," said Jane, "shall we raise a glass?"

By the end of the evening they had raised several glasses each.

"Where was you friend, Molly, in all this," asked Lydia. "I was hoping to meet her."

"I don't know," said Gertrude. "I should call her and see if she's home yet. I think she's not far. I can feel her calling me." Gertrude settled herself more comfortably into the corner of the sofa and allowed her attention to drift. "I'm here, Molly," she mumbled.

"Humph, it's about time," said Molly. "I've been sitting here watching to you all guzzling Angus' rum without so much as a please and thank you."

"Where have you been? And we were enjoying it," said Gertrude. "We weren't guzzling."

"Guzzling," said Molly. "I was wishing for a sip. It was the last bottle."

"You can have the last in my glass if you'd like, but I warn you, it's pretty strong stuff."

"Thanks, but we only pretend over here. You know that."

"Yes," said Gertrude. "So where were you all summer?"

"After we last talked, Larry and I went to Hawaii and spent the summer sunbathing and surfing and visiting with the gods and goddesses. They're all friends of ours and we hadn't seen them for a while. We had some lovely luaus. We went there from the Bahamas." Molly hummed one of the tunes she learned. "Mm, we only intended to stay a couple of weeks but it was so lovely we decided to stay for the rest of the summer since you didn't really need me."

"So you and Larry are quite the item now, huh?"

"We have been for a long time. Occasionally it was on your side and sometimes it has been here, if we've both been here at the same time. I see you finally tracked down Julia's coat. She's ecstatic over the thing. Personally I've always thought that furs were too much, never mind the poor foxes that were killed for them and dog meat. If the dogs had known where their meat was coming from they would have been horrified. Eating one of their own."

"So Julia got her coat. How'd she lose it in the first place?"

"She hung it in her dressing room and someone stole it during her time on stage. She forgot to lock her door so it was sort of her own fault. She got it from that fancy guy she was seeing at the time, that Mr. Argent."

Larry wafted in wearing his ancient hat with the big red plume. "That coat has been all over the world in the intervening years. No one knew where it had gone. It was passed from hand to hand over the years. It went to France just before World War One. It was sold for food at one point, times were so tough. Then some Frenchman, I forget his name, saw it for what it was in a second hand shop in Marseilles."

Molly interrupted. "He bought it and had it cleaned for his mistress. She wore it while she was with him but then his wife got wind of his little dalliance and confronted the mistress and took the coat right off her back. I understand it was quite a row; a lot of hair-pulling and swearing. The mistress was better at it than the wife but the wife saved her breath for the fight and managed to get the coat away from the mistress. She wore it for a very long time and left it to her daughter in her will. The daughter, Marie, wanted to have it brought up to date and tried to do it herself but only managed to get it apart. It ended up in her attic in pieces."

"I lived in that house for awhile after the war," said Larry, "but by that time the coat was long forgotten about. When her granddaughter was clearing out the house after she died, the granddaughter found this old coat and took it to a furrier to have it put back together again, but then she took ill and the coat stayed with the furrier until Jane's grandfather came along just at the end of

World War One and bought it from the furrier to bring home to your grandmother." Larry paused for breath.

"Your grandmother looked the coat all over and discovered the tag inside with Julia's name on it," said Molly. "She was quite gleeful about having found the coat and never told Julia that she had found it, and wanted to get back at her for a number of the nasty tricks Julia had pulled over the course of their lifetimes, in particular for taking away the lead in *La Bohème*. That would have been the making of Jane's grandmother's career. So she hid it in the space behind the new mantel along with the album of photos and newspaper clippings and never told anyone about it."

"Grandma was also kind of miffed with Grandpa too," said Larry. "Julia appeared just after Angus and Freddie were married and Julia made quite a play for Angus. Grandma had to lay down the law to Grandpa, so she said. Grandpa was just a simple farmer and was easily dazzled by the big opera star that he thought Julia was. He was still pretty young."

"Did Julia ever find out where her coat was?" asked Gertrude.

"After Grandma made her transition she ran into Julia and told her what she'd done," said Molly. "There was an awful fight. Worse than the one in

France. Both Grandma and Julia ended up in solitary for a week and then they were banished to opposite ends of the universe. They haven't seen each other since."

"Just as well," mumbled Gertrude. "Why was the coat so important to Julia?"

"Because Mr. Argent gave it to her," said Larry. "I think he was the only man Julia ever truly loved. She would have given up her career for him if he'd asked. He just never asked. His family had other plans for him, and marrying a common, mediocre opera singer wasn't part of those plans."

"Well, that's quite a story," said Gertrude. "So are you and Molly done gallivanting?"

"For now," said Larry. "Jim's got a big research project on and he's been guiding that through Mary Ann. They still work very closely together whenever they can. I think Mary Ann is ever hopeful that their relationship will develop beyond just friendship."

"I see. That must be why Mary Ann has been so unavailable lately. Julia didn't like her a bit."

"No, she didn't. Your friend's power's are waning. She's having more and more difficulty contacting this side and she doesn't recover as fast as she used to. She still does good research on your side though and can be very useful still. On the other hand, your powers are increasing and your boy is going to be phenomenal when he reaches maturity. You'll even have a hard time keeping up with him. You'll have to guide him carefully and not let him squander his ability on silly readings for his friends."

"Watch out for a kid named Tony. He won't be a good influence. He has some skill too but he has never learned to use it properly. He got in with the wrong crowd on this side so they sent him over there. Roddy doesn't know him yet but he'll meet him in the next year or so," said Larry.

"What about Charlotte?"

"So you finally named her," said Molly. "Pretty. She's going to give you a run for your money too. She's as able as Roddy. She won't realize it until she's older of course, but you'll still have to be a strong parent for her."

Gertrude looked alarmed. "Will I be having any more psychic kids?"

"None that I can see. You'll have your hands full with the ones you've got. And then the grandchildren! Whew! You're in for a wild ride. Gotta go. Don't tell Mary Ann what I said. She doesn't need to know. She'll find out soon enough."

Larry slowly lost strength in Gertrude's awareness.

"Larry was chatty this evening," said Gertrude in her mind. "He's usually so short on conversation. The vacation must have done him good."

"He's happy just now. He just had word from the

elders the other day that he and I are going to be on this side for a few more generations. We work well together." Molly smiled a secret smile. "And you're going to need all the help you can get." She began to fade from Gertrude's inner vision.

Gertrude stirred in her chair and opened her eyes. "Did you guys hear any of that?"

"Some," said Jane. "Something about a fight and World War One and Grandpa."

"You didn't get very much," said Gertrude. She related most of the story to the others. "So that's the story of the coat." She stretched her slender arms above her head. "I get stiff when the session is long."

"What I don't understand is why Molly and Larry are so talkative and Julia can only whisper and not very long at that?" said Lydia.

"Molly and Larry are old, experienced spirits and they know how to keep the energy up long enough to have a conversation. Julia was new to it all and really didn't know what to do except to scare people. Occasionally she could put a coherent sentence together, then she'd lose energy. I was giving her a lot of my energy just to keep her here long enough to get the little I did from her. It was exhausting."

"What about Grandma and Grandpa?" asked Jane. "I know Grandpa never had very much to say to you in trance, but I wonder why not?"

"That's not really surprising," said Gertrude, "he still hasn't lost the earthly habit of keeping his business to himself. They're not very interested in Julia and her fur coats and love intrigues anymore. They just wanted to be sure that she couldn't harm you," said Gertrude. "Once they knew that I would be here figuring things out they just stayed in the background."

"How did the coat disappear?" asked Ian.

"Everything is energy," said Gertrude. "We're just one great boiling mass of energy with forms to fill for however long. Physics is finally getting the hang of it."

"That's too deep for me," said Jane. "Can you guys put the surround back in place, please."

"You'll have to get the vacuum out and suck up all that energy from the closet along with the dust," said Gertrude.

"I'll put the kettle on," said Lydia.

They all gathered around the kitchen table to review the day's happening.

"We've had quite an adventure this summer," said Jane, "and I haven't even told you what Ian and I did this afternoon."

"So what did you do?" asked Gertrude. She settled herself in the chair closest to the stove. "I get so chilled when I trance." She looked at Jane.

"We got the door in the cellar opened. I'll bet you can't guess what else we found?"

"I'm too tired to guess. Spill."

"We found more of Grandpa's still. At least I think that's what it was. It's all in pieces in the room behind the old boiler."

"Oh," said Gertrude. "It was there too?"

"I'll be interested to find out if that chest full of money is still worth anything," said Gertrude.

"Jane and I are taking a bill to the bank tomorrow to see," said Ian.

"Well, that's really exciting," said Gertrude. "I can't wait to tell Don."

"Don't tell anyone else, though," said Jane. "Whenever there's any money involved people seem to come out of the woodwork trying to cash in."

"Yeah," said Ian, "I've always felt sorry for lottery winners. Free-loaders never seem to leave them alone."

"You'll be able to fix this place up to its original state," said Lydia.

"Let's not count chickens," said Jane. "The money may not be worth very much, if anything, anymore."

In fact, the money was worth a great deal more than it was originally. It had antique value as well as having grown in value intrinsically. Jane and Ian sat in Ian's truck and discussed the matter.

"We'll have to get the bank to send an armoured car for this one," said Ian. "I don't fancy driving to town with a chest full of money in the back of my truck."

"Nor I," said Jane. "I never realized how tiring it would be to have this much money."

"It's a great responsibility," agreed Ian. "I think you need to give a lot of serious thought to how you're going to handle it."

"I suppose I'd better get myself a lawyer and an investment broker. I don't think the bank would like me to just let the money sit in my savings account." She fell silent and pondered her next move.

Ian pulled into the road to the old lighthouse. "Maybe a little sea air is what you need." He drove down the lane and stopped facing the Northumberland Strait. Sun sparkled on the water and the day was September warm. The odour of sea and dry grasses filled the cabin. "C'mere, you." Ian held out his arms to Jane. "D'you realize this is the first we've been truly alone since we met this time around?"

Jane slid across the seat and snuggled into Ian's arms. "I guess it is. I haven't really had much time to think about us at all. Lydia was always there and she was always match making about us and I've been fending her off and trying to keep her distracted. And then there was all that ghostly stuff going on, and the dogs, and all that cleaning and repairing and on, and on. It seemed never ending. Mind you, I'm glad that Lydia was there. By myself I would have been so spooked by all of it that I'd have gone running back to town and locked the doors behind myself and probably never come out here again."

"Well, I'm glad she kept you from doing all that," said Ian. "I'm glad that school is starting and I'll at least see you in the evenings now and again."

"Mm," said Jane. "It'll be nice."

"It'll be nice to find out if we have anything solid between us," said Ian.

Jane sat up and turned to look at Ian. "I think we do," said Jane. "It never occurred to me that we didn't. I was just waiting to see how things developed. You're very slow sometimes. I've also had a bad relationship experience when I was in teacher's college in Truro so I wasn't eager to go too fast."

"Tell me about it."

"Sometime," said Jane and slid over to her place in the passenger seat.

"I guess it's time to go home," said Ian. He leaned forward to start the truck.